"I'M GONNA DIE..."

The cop swore again, then turned the nozzle, and a short, smooth jet of flame erupted. "Last chance, friend," he yelled into the dumpster. "I'm not going to stand here all night."

He raised his arm, the nozzle pointed, the flame a foot and a half long by now, and I braced one sneaker against the corner of the dumpster and pushed myself sideways. I guess he wasn't expecting heroics, and I knocked him off balance. Not down, just off balance.

He staggered, then whipped the hose around, and the flame struck the dumpster wall and split into tongues. He came at me, slowly, his lips drawn back, his face dancing with shadows, swiveling that nozzle, aiming it at my stomach, and I thought, I'm gonna die. *I'm gonna die!*

Other Avon Books in the
U.S.S.A.™ Series

BOOK 2 *by S.N. Lewitt*

Coming Soon
BOOK 3 *by S.C. Sykes*

TOM DE HAVEN is the author of *Funny Papers,* which *Saturday Review* hailed as "dazzlingly inventive... a terrific book." His other books include *Freaks Amour* and *Jersey Luck.* Tom De Haven teaches creative writing at Hofstra University and lives with his wife and two daughters in New Jersey.

U.S.S.A.™ BOOK I

Tom De Haven

A GLC Book

AVON
PUBLISHERS OF BARD, CAMELOT, DISCUS AND FLARE BOOKS

For Jessie and Kate

U.S.S.A.® BOOK 1 is an original publication of Avon Books. This work has never before appeared in book form. This work is a novel. Any similarity to actual persons or events is purely coincidental.

AVON BOOKS
A division of
The Hearst Corporation
1790 Broadway
New York, New York 10019

Published by arrangement with General Licensing Company, Inc.
Library of Congress Catalog Card Number: 86-91605
ISBN: 0-380-75180-1

Developed by Byron Preiss and Dan Weiss
Edited by David M. Harris
Cover painting by Paul Rivoche

First Avon Printing: February 1987

Printed in the U.S.A.

K-R 10 9 8 7 6 5 4 3 2 1

Chapter 1

I should've trusted my gut and stayed away from the Bazaar.

That evening after supper I'd gone over to Lincoln Park with Mike Fromkin to shoot baskets. Around seven-thirty it got dark, so we called it quits and drifted off the courts. Drank and squirted each other at the water fountain, then flopped down on a small hill by the duck pond. There weren't any ducks, and hadn't been since I was ten or eleven. Mike lay flat on his back, grinning lazily at the sky. The clouds were big and bunched-up, and some birds flew past in a loose V-formation. We watched the moon come up and turn yellow.

"What's today?" Mike asked me all of a sudden.

"The nineteenth," I said. "You need the month too? It's April."

"Don't be wise. I meant day of the week."

"Wednesday."

"Bazaar night."

"Forget it," I told him. "I don't have any money."

"Scared?" he asked, sitting up and giving me a lopsided grin.

"Yeah, right."

"So come on, then. You don't need any money." He got up, squeezing the basketball with his palms. It popped out and bounced. I grabbed it. "We'll just take a quick look," he said, "then go straight home."

"All right." But I was reluctant. I wasn't scared, just—just reluctant. And like I say, I should've trusted my gut.

It was only a five-minute walk from the park to the brass foundry, way down at the weedy end of Grant Street. We climbed the fence and jumped down on the other side, into high, scratchy grass. It was full dark by then, and the foundry, which had to be a hundred years old, looked real creep-show. A long, red, half-collapsed heap of bricks without a roof. There'd been a fire there five or six years ago, and the place had never been rebuilt. One less industry in Sandersville, and fifty fewer jobs.

We crept down to the far end of the building, and it was so quiet that I thought maybe the Bazaar wasn't happening tonight or else the dealers had moved it someplace else. But then we turned the corner, and about twenty, twenty-five kids froze like rabbits. When they saw it was cool, though—that it was only Mike and me, they all relaxed and resumed their business. And their business, of course, was checking out suitcases and beach blankets full of rock records and prerecorded tapes, music that you couldn't buy legally anymore, thanks to the new military government. Most of the stuff, I'd heard, was smuggled down from Canada, or else came into Ohio from some pressing plants out West that the federal police force—the New Cops—hadn't found out about yet.

I stooped and checked out several records. Some were used and some were still in their shrink-wrap. Six months earlier, you could've bought any of them everywhere. Now you had to sneak around behind the brass foundry. It was funny, but it wasn't really, if you know what I mean. The Government was big on Moral Renewal, and practically every time you turned on the TV, you'd see some guy or woman with thin lips spouting about how loud music was socially irresponsible. Loud music, weird clothes, trade unions, sex before marriage, drug use, and Japanese electronics.

I recognized most of the kids at the Bazaar—they were from the high school, mostly—and I said hey to half a dozen of them, while Mike snooped at a blanket and asked the dealer, "How much for this Springsteen?" The guy said "Forty," and I heard Mike suck hard on his front teeth, make a sizzling noise.

I went and leaned against the foundry wall. I was feeling a little bit nervous, I have to admit. At school lately we'd been hearing about record and T-shirt busts, and about Dark Concerts that had been raided by the New Cops. A Dark Concert was what everybody called it when some rock band the Government didn't like sneaked into town and played music somewhere soundproof with blackout curtains on the windows. Things had turned so weird, so really weird and scary since last January, since the Joint Chiefs of Staff suspended the Constitution and took over. Took over everything. One day on the radio there'd been rock and roll and News at Six; next day, official bulletins and Beethoven sonatas. Weird.

Hunkered down near the corner of the foundry, just a few feet away from me, was a fat kid with bright red hair. He was rifling through some compact discs piled in a ratty-looking steamer trunk. Clamped in his teeth was a penlight, to see the merchandise better. "Trick Oyster!" he exclaimed in a loud whisper. "You got the new Trick Oyster. All right! I'd kill to own this record."

The dealer laughed. "You don't have to kill anybody, just give me thirty-five bucks."

The kid went for the deal, and I watched him count out the money—three tens and five singles. He took the disc and pressed it close to his heart like he loved it. Mike came over then and asked me if I was ready to leave. I told him yeah, sure, but then suddenly—there, there, over there, and there—humongous yellow lights blazed on, and an amplified voice said: "Everybody stay right where you are. You're under arrest."

Mike flung his basketball and we both took off running. So did everybody else. And for a couple of seconds it was completely nuts, it was like some comedy routine—everybody slamming into everybody else, kids tripping, sprawling, cursing, and yelling.

As soon as I turned the corner of the foundry, I saw maybe a dozen silhouettes directly ahead of us—New Cops standing where we'd come over the fence not ten minutes ago. More lights went on, so bright they blinded me. I spun around, hissed at Mike, "Stay with me," and ran a zigzag through the weedy grounds. I scrambled toward a stand of dense evergreen trees, then dove and scuttled on all fours, crawling underneath the bottom branches on my belly.

Mike and I huddled there, behind the trees and against the fence, trying to slow our breathing. Finally I looked back.

There must've been a dozen New Cops, at least, darting every which way with clubs raised, with clubs swinging, with clubs coming down, hard, on elbows, shoulder blades, and skulls. Some kids, the youngest-looking ones, had given up already and were standing in a circle—like they'd been told to—with their hands joined together. I saw a dealer down on his knees, his back bent and his fingers twitching, tearing at the grass. I watched him vomit, try to stand, wobble, vomit again, totter, and fall. Then I heard a loud swoosh and saw a New Cop turn a flamethrower on a suitcase full of tapes. He turned it next on the beach towels, oozing about a hundred and fifty albums in one second flat. Mike whispered, "They're gonna find us," and I told him to shut up, just shut up. My shirt was sticking to me and my heart was trying to blow itself out of my chest.

Then somebody was grunting nearby, and we crouched down tighter. A moment later, the fat kid who'd bought the Trick Oyster started wiggling under the branches. He was halfway to us when a New Cop spotted him and snatched him by the ankles. The kid's eyes bugged open, and he started flopping and thrashing, same as a fish on a dock, trying to break free. But the cop held on. I reached and grabbed the kid's wrists, to pull him toward me. But the cop was stronger. The kid screamed like he was being torn in half. Then he was gone, dragged back onto the foundry grounds.

"Let's go!" I told Mike. "Now!"

We burst out of the trees, branches slapping our faces, and started running again. There was a seven-foot-high dumpster straight ahead, and I meant to duck behind it, catch my breath, think for a second. But Mike had a different, stupid idea. Before I could stop him, he'd clambered up the side of the dumpster and rolled over the top. He grunted as he hit a cushion of paper, then I heard him digging around, burrowing in.

A second later, I felt a heavy, clamping pressure on my right shoulder, then a sharp pain in my lower back. The jolt sent me flying into the metal dumpster, and if I hadn't turned my face just then, I probably would've broken half my teeth. But I only ended up with a split cheek. I tried to raise a hand to squeeze the cut closed, but the New Cop slapped it away. "Don't give me any crap. Where's your pal—inside?"

I shook my head no, and the cop kneed me

again, in the same spot. I saw bright flecks of light, and the pain rocketed straight into my skull.

"Keep your hands behind your back," said the cop, "and your forehead against the dumpster." I did what he told me, but looked sideways, so I could see him. He was wearing a helmet with the infrared visor snapped down, and he had a big paunch that strained against his black leather uniform tunic. He carried a flamethrower strapped across his back, like an Aqua-lung. The hose and nozzle dragged the ground. He banged a fist against the dumpster and shouted, "You in there! You got three seconds to drag your ass out. Before I burn it out."

He swore under his breath, then stood on his toes, clamped his fingers over the edge of the dumpster, and lifted himself. He peered over the top. In those two seconds, I could've made another run for it. But I didn't. I couldn't leave Mike.

The cop swung the flamethrower around in front of him, yanked on the hose, and caught the nozzle in a gloved fist. "Lot of paper in there, sonny boy," he called. "And if you're at the bottom of it, you're gonna get mighty crisp mighty fast. Come on out, huh? I'm losing my patience. Come out!"

But Mike didn't.

The cop swore again, then turned the nozzle, half-turned it, and a short, smooth jet of flame erupted. It reflected off his visor and made a quivering shadow on the bottom half of his face. There was a mole on his chin the size of a cashew. "Last chance, friend," he yelled into the dumpster. "I'm not going to stand here all night."

He raised his arm, the nozzle pointed, the flame a foot and a half long by now, and I braced one foot against the corner of the dumpster and pushed myself sideways. I guess he wasn't expecting heroics, and I knocked him off balance. Not down, just off balance. He staggered to his right, then whipped the hose around, and the flame struck the dumpster wall, split into tongues. He came at me then, slowly, his lips drawn back, his face dancing with shadows, and he was swiveling that nozzle from side to side, aiming it at my stomach, and I dodged, dodged and backstepped. And thought, I'm gonna die. I'm gonna die!

But before he could burn me, there was a loud and crazy war whoop—Mike diving through the air like Batman and landing square on the cop's back. They crashed down in a heap. The fire spit across the ground, igniting grass and scraps of old paper, and scorching the cop's hand. He howled and rolled, and kept on rolling. Mike passed me on the run and hooked me by an arm, practically lifted me up and dragged me with him. By then, other cops were charging at us, and it was pandemonium city all over again. Up ahead, I heard loud clashing and rattling, the sound of kids' bodies hitting a chain-link fence and scrambling up. Mike got there first but waited for me, then we scaled it together, jumped together, bounced together, then ran like hell. Down Grant to Harrison, along Harrison and through a weed lot to Van Buren, where we slowed finally, then dragged ourselves behind a dark Exxon station and collapsed.

"Got any other fun plans for tonight?" I asked him when I could catch my breath again, but he wasn't in the mood for wisecracks.

Chapter 2

Two weeks after the Bazaar scare, the birds arrived in Sandersville.

I got up that morning at twenty to eight, same time I always did, and put on black jeans and a Murder of Crows Tour '94 T-shirt, then went downstairs and had a couple of cinnamon Pop Tarts. The weather was cloudy and it looked like maybe later it might rain.

Mom was still asleep, but I didn't mind and I didn't wake her. Lately she'd been feeling low, hardly ever smiling the way she used to and never going near her typewriter. She slept late and went to bed early, and she wouldn't read the newspapers or watch TV. Dad was always saying to me, or giving me a look that said, "Be patient, Eddie, she'll be all right, just leave her alone." So I did.

I left her alone. Dad had been away since Tuesday. He was due back Sunday.

I finished breakfast, turned off the kitchen radio—the spokesman on the National Network said that everything was okay, God bless us, in the United Secure States of America—and then I got ready to leave for school, jamming my gym stuff, a few books, and a couple of homework diskettes into my shoulder bag. Finally I grabbed my jacket and left.

I was seventeen and licensed to drive, but juniors didn't have parking privileges, so I walked to school, taking Roosevelt to Ridge, then Ridge all the way across town to President Street. It was windy, and the wind, as it usually did, carried a heavy scent of cat food from the cannery on Railroad Avenue.

I started thinking about how great it was going to be when school was over, in just another month. I was thinking it'd be neat, come June, to take a ride with Mike and B.J. out to Panther Lake to swim, to rent a canoe, and then maybe tip it over for a goof. To hike through Rhodes's Property, then zoom around the amusement park.

Thinking about all that made the walk go quick. And I hardly noticed the Army jeep sitting out in front of City Hall. I mean, I noticed it, but nothing happened. Usually I'd see it and something would twist inside me and I'd clench my teeth, which wasn't a great idea since I had a couple of small cavities and they hurt when I did that. At the moment, the town was missing its Mayor. He'd gone to Washington for a meeting and never came back.

I got to school about twenty minutes after eight and was dumping stuff into my locker when somebody called me. Without turning around, I knew who it was, and I wasn't glad. I slammed the locker shut, glanced over my shoulder, and said, "Hey, Will."

Will Farmer was standing there behind me in the corridor, flanked by three guys. Two of them were seniors—football players but second-stringers—and the other kid was slightly built with lots of blackheads and a real weasely smirk, a sophomore. The second-stringers had their arms folded like bottle genies. The weasel was carrying a stack of mimeo paper that smelled sickly-sweet. Will told him, "Give Eddie one of those."

I already knew what it was going to be, and I wasn't interested, but I didn't feel like making any big production, so I took the flyer. It was still damp, and said: "Join The Young Patriots! Membership Meeting Today. Room 001. 3:15. Be Part of the Great Renewal!"

I said thanks, folded it in half, then turned to leave.

"So?" said Will, touching my elbow. "You going to be there?"

I looked into his face, then down at his fingers, still squeezing me. He let go, flashing me that famous big smile of his. And I was thinking, We used to be friends? Amazing. But things change. All kinds of things change, all the time.

"You going to be there?" he asked me again.

"I don't know," I said, still not wanting to make any big production. "Probably not. I'm kind of busy."

"Yeah? Doing what?"

"That's none of your business," I told him, beginning to feel tight across my chest. "I'm just kind of busy."

"That's too bad," said Will, backing off. "We'll miss you."

We stared at each other, and for a second, for just a second, I saw a familiar, teasing glint in Will's eyes, and the corners of his mouth turned up, and then I said to myself, Yeah, we used to be friends. We used to be good friends. Best friends. But then his face turned stony again and he lifted one shoulder in a kind of half shrug, and he was So Important, So Full of Himself again, and I hated his guts. But I felt bad about it. Deep down, I felt real bad about it.

The first bell rang before I got to Homeroom, and I came charging in, figuring to find everybody seated and Mr. Kantrowitz reading the general announcements. Instead, the kids of 3A were all standing around talking or else looking out the window. And Mr. K wasn't there. His shabby leather briefcase wasn't on the desk, and neither were his black-covered attendance book or his morning's glazed donut, which was kind of his trademark and something of a joke around the high school. It was a relief, not being late, not being marked late. Not that it was any big deal, you know, but still, I just didn't like red checks alongside my name.

I dropped my shoulder bag on a desk, said hey to Teddy Grimmeyer, Al Foye, Scott Regan, and Mary Doran, then looked around for B.J., hoping she wasn't absent. And no, she wasn't, so the day had potential. She was over at the window with the Kelting twins, who were pointing to something outside. B.J. squinted, straining to see what they were trying to show her. Even with her glasses on, she was nearsighted, which was pretty crazy when you think about it. I mean, change your prescription, girl—right? B.J. hated wearing glasses, said they made her look ugly and dull. She was wrong. But then, I was prejudiced.

I squeezed behind a couple of desks to join her and the Keltings, who were identical twins but didn't look it. Patty had her hair cut real short last winter, and Lynn had put on a whole lot of weight. And they never dressed the same. B.J. saw me coming. If we weren't in public, she probably would've kissed me, but she only smiled and said, "Hey, Eddie." Then she looked at my T-shirt and frowned. "I hope you don't get in trouble, wearing that."

"They're not on the list," I said, alarmed for a second.

"You sure?"

I nodded, but suddenly I wasn't, and felt a spark of panic. But Lynn Kelting said B.J. was wrong and I was right. You couldn't wear Billy Panter shirts, or Sunday Orphans shirts, or Backsliders shirts, or any shirts, buttons, or fingernail transfers naming any group or singer that had performed at last February's Concerts for Conscience in Detroit and Atlanta. But Murder of Crows was okay, she said. Their songs were only about love. "And besides," she said, "Bernie Heebert's dad is a colonel in the army."

"Who's Bernie Heebert?" B.J. wanted to know.

"Lead singer in the Crows," Lynn replied, by now sick of talking about my shirt. That made two of us. I'd already started wishing I hadn't worn the stupid thing. I didn't like the Crows that much anyway.

B.J. changed the subject. "We've been looking at birds," she said with a self-conscious giggle. She cocked her head toward the windowpane, her blond hair swinging as she did.

"Birds?" I said. That was weird.

"Those sparrows over there," said Patty Kelting. "Aren't they sort of big?"

I took a squint where the girls were pointing. About twenty chunky-looking sparrows with black and white crown stripes sat all in a row on some telephone wires across the street from school. Their heads were moving from side to side, slowly and all at the same time. Twenty bird heads looking to the right, to the left, moving down, moving up. That's what struck me as weird, not that they were bigger than they should've been, which they were.

Just then, a brown Ford Rex came along President Street and veered suddenly into the school parking lot. Immediately, two of the birds swooped down past the Rex, one on each side. Then they flew back up and perched on the wire again, exactly where they'd been before.

I looked at B.J. and she looked at me, and we

both made what's-going-on faces. But before we could talk about it, Patty Kelting said hey.

I glanced around and there was a stranger standing behind Mr. Kantrowitz's desk. He wore a dark gray unconstructed jacket, a white shirt, and a skinny black leather tie. He had crinkly brown hair cut short, a narrow V-shaped head, and a small red mouth tipped up in a small red smile.

Everybody stopped talking and waited for him to say something. And what he finally said, in a deep, Southern-flavored voice that didn't fit his body or his face, was this: "My name is Mr. Laudermilch. If you'd all take your seats, we can get started." He checked his watch and frowned. "We have only four minutes till your first class. Sit." He narrowed his eyes and took out a roll book.

"Affinito," he said, "Bonner, Boyle, Brezicki . . ." Hands shot up all around the room and voices said present. I started biting on a knuckle, and bit so hard finally that I almost broke the skin. I felt sort of—I tell you, I don't know what I felt, exactly. Queasy, like. Something was wrong. But that's stupid, I thought, rubbing and pinching the teeth marks out of my skin. Stupid. Kantrowitz was absent—he could have the flu, or something—and this Laudermilch was only subbing. That's all. That's all. Yeah, right. And maybe the Mayor also had the flu.

"Ludlow."

"Here," I said.

"McFadden, Nilan, Ocasion, Pendleton . . ."

I looked out the window, and the sparrows had all flown away.

The bell rang for change of class, first period, and on my way out, I happened to glance over into the corner of the room, where the U.S. flag used to hang. It had been taken down in February, along with every other American flag at school, the same week the Joint Chiefs decided the country needed another, stronger name. Temporarily, they said. Just till we citizens toughened our moral fiber and the troublemakers in Iran, Iraq, Saudi Arabia, and Mexico cried uncle.

B.J. walked me down the hall. I looked at the piece of yellow yarn tied in her hair. Real pretty. There was a smudge, a thumbprint on one of the lenses of her eyeglasses. I noticed the stupidest things, sometimes. "That's a relief," she said.

"What is?"

"That Mr. Kantrowitz is absent. It means no quiz."

"Yeah," I said, seeing one of those Young Patriot flyers tacked up on the Biology Lab bulletin board. "But who are you kidding? You would've got a 98," I said, jabbing a finger between her ribs, teasing her.

We separated at the end of the hall—she was going to Computer Programming and I was going to English, upstairs. "See you at lunch," I called after her.

"If you get there first," she said, "pick me up large french fries, would you? And a hamburger, not a cheeseburger. And if they have those chocolate donuts, a chocolate donut."

"You're going to get fat."

She smiled and waved.

All around me, kids were trooping down the halls, griping or clowning, and I cut across them and trudged upstairs.

Walking into class, I said hi to Mr. Graham, the teacher, then nodded to Will Farmer, sitting in his regular seat at the back of the room. He was reading a paperback copy of *All Quiet on the Western Front.* There was an empty desk beside his in the next aisle, but I passed on that one and sat up front, next to Mandy Gould. Her perfume was great.

Mr. Graham stood at the door till the late bell rang, then he yanked it shut and strolled to his desk. He used to be the school's most casual dresser, always wearing blue workshirts or lumberjack shirts, jeans or corduroy pants, sometimes an old sport coat, but not often. Lately, though, he'd been dressing in brand-new suits and spiffy ties. He used to wear a small earring in his left ear, but no longer. And now he wore a 119 button on his lapel, every day. So did several other teachers, of course. So did the principal, the assistant principal. So did a lot of kids, for that matter. But Mr. Graham was the first to show up with one. Like, it was hardly a week after the military coup, and there he was, in a new haircut, a new suit, and wearing that button. One nineteen, for January the nineteenth, the day that everything changed.

Some kids thought Graham was a snitch, but I didn't know. He could've been, I guess. Or not. I hoped not.

He was a short, broad-shouldered guy in his late twenties, with sandy-colored hair and a thick mustache. Nobody knew too much about him, really. Other teachers you always heard about. You knew where they lived, what town they'd grown up in, if they were married or single or divorced, if they had any kids. But nobody knew much about Graham. In that respect, he was like Mr. Kantrowitz. But only in that respect. Kantrowitz was loose, friendly, and just about the smartest teacher at the school. He'd once showed us an article about Sacco and Vanzetti that he'd written for *American Heritage* magazine. He'd never worn a 119 button. And he never would, he'd said a couple of times. Immediately after General Sawchuk replaced the President, Mr. K'd spent three classes telling us about the politics that had led up to it, asking our opinions, all that kind of stuff. But on the third day, Mr. Belton, the principal, had dropped in unexpectedly, and the very next morning Kantrowitz had gone right back to teaching us about Jacksonian democracy.

"Let's finish up our discussion of *All Quiet on the Western Front,*" Mr. Graham was saying. "Shall we?" He picked up a stick of chalk and wrote one word on the blackboard: Patriotism. He underscored it twice, then boxed it, then turned around and smiled at the class. "What are some of your thoughts on that?" he asked, running his eyes around the room. He had small, piercing eyes that could really make you feel uncomfortable.

"Our heroes in this novel," he said. "Those German boys, those soldiers. They loved their country, correct? And they went out and fought a war when their government told them to." He looked around, flipping his chalk up in the air and catching it, flipping it up and catching it. "How about this, then? Is patriotism—the love of one's country—always the same thing as the love of one's government?"

I was thinking that I liked class much better when we discussed characterization and plot. Or, like, when we spent a whole period trying to decide whether Ophelia was pregnant or not when she drowned herself.

"Mr. Bonner," said Mr. Graham. "What if you didn't think that your government was legitimate? What if you disagreed fundamentally with your government? Should you say no to it in time of war?"

Jackie Bonner, the best Ping-Pong player in Sandersville High, gave a little shrug.

"Donald Rider," said Mr. Graham, with a sigh. "Would you refuse to go to war if you believed that your government was unjust or illegitimate?"

"No," Donny Rider said quickly, without a second's hesitation, and I swear I saw him glance back at Will Farmer, who was sitting with his hands folded almost primly on the edge of his desk.

"Is it patriotism, then, to do what your country demands, even when, to your way of thinking, the demand is wrong?" Mr. Graham had strolled down the aisle and was staring at Donny.

"I don't know if it's patriotism," said Donny, "but I know that if you don't go, it's treason. And you'd end up in prison with a—"

"So what you're saying . . . is this what you're saying: that patriotism isn't so much love of country, it's fear of punishment?"

"Yes," said Donny. Then, "No," said Donny one second later. Then he frowned and shook his head. Some kids laughed. I looked around at Will. He'd slumped down in his seat. He raised his fingers slowly to his lips, then smirked behind them. I felt like belting him, honest to God. Even when he was my friend, I never could stand that superior attitude of his, that smugness, that I'm-smarter-than-you stuff.

Graham never asked me any questions, and I sort of drifted off, doodling mentally. I loved my country, I told myself. Sure. But hey, which country was my country, anyway? The U.S.A.? Or the U.S.S.A.? Were they both the same country, or not? The U.S.A. didn't arrest kids just for going to a rock concert, didn't send the secret police to bust your head and practically incinerate you if you wanted to buy a record. But the U.S.S.A. did. And it shut newspapers down and folded magazines and censored movies and produced the only news that you could get. And yeah, I was afraid of the Government. I was afraid of the U.S.S.A. So did that mean I wasn't patriotic? Or that I was? I was giving myself a headache, and a stomachache, and my fingers hurt from being clenched so tight.

When there were only a few more minutes left before the bell, I looked around at Will Farmer again, and he was furiously jotting something down in a small blue spiral pad. It wasn't his class notebook—that was lying open on top of his desk. He caught me staring, and as soon as he did, he grinned and flipped the pad closed. Then he stuck it in his shirt pocket.

I wondered what he was writing down.

Chapter 3

After English came Trig, and after Trig came Gym, and down in the locker room, I spotted Mike Fromkin frowning over his padlock. He'd forgotten his combination again! He'd only had the same lock for two years already. I watched him twirl the dial, yank at the shackle, then scratch his head when it refused to pop open. He twisted up his mouth and laughed at himself.

Meanwhile, all around us, guys were banging doors open, changing clothes, racing out. I could hear basketballs start to bounce on the gym floor and slam off backboards.

"You need some help?" I asked Mike, walking over and grinning my face off.

He looked at me and sighed.

"Twenty-seven right, twelve left, twenty-two right," I told him.

"Hey Eddie, not so loud," he said, putting a silencing finger to his lips. I had to laugh. Like, what'd he keep in there that anybody'd want to steal? "So how you doing, Eddie?" he said, dialing the combination.

"Good, I guess," I told him. Back at my own locker again, I said hey to Jackie Bonner and Scott Regan as they trotted by. They called hey to Mike, but he barely nodded at them. He'd changed into his running shorts and was standing at his locker, reading something now, something that he'd found inside, that somebody must have pushed through a ventilation slit. His big, usually wide-open face suddenly darkened. He crumpled up the sheet of paper and whipped it away, hard. It bounced off a locker. Finally he put on his sneakers and T-shirt.

"Mike," I called. I had one foot up on the bench and was tying my laces. "Kantrowitz ever get in?"

Mike had History second period.

He shook his head, then began to say something, but didn't. He finished changing and we walked together through the locker room. When we came to an aisle of lockers with nobody around, he stopped me and whispered, "Somebody says Mr. K got arrested last night."

And my gut sank.

"You sure?"

"No, I just heard."

"Who from?"

"It doesn't matter, Eddie. He just heard it from somebody else, who heard it from somebody else."

"Arrested for what?"

Mike shrugged. "And hey, Eddie? We had this substitute."

"Laudermilch. I had him for Homeroom."

Mike nodded. "He's no teacher."

"Boring?"

"No, I mean—" Mike looked around again. Man, he was more suspicious about things than anybody else I knew, except maybe my mother. "I mean," he continued in a quieter voice, "I mean, I don't think he's a real sub. I think he's, you know, a spy."

"For who?"

"Come on, Eddie, be real. He could be a New Cop."

"You be real," I said. "Let's go play some basketball."

"Do you think Kantrowitz was really arrested?"

"Hey, Mike," I said, "you're the one who told me that. How should I know?" And I felt sick, thinking: arrested.

As we approached the gym doors, one of the second-string ball players I'd seen earlier with Will Farmer stepped out from behind a locker. Ugly guy, sneering at us. Where'd he learn to pull that kind of face? From Stu Haring movies? You could tell, here was a kid who'd always root for the bone-breakers, the bad guys. He sneered, like I say, then waved a wrinkled flyer at Mike. "People go to all the trouble of printing these things, the least you can do is show some respect," he said.

Mike flushed angrily and cut his eyes to one side. Then he grabbed the flyer from the second-string goon and stormed off, banging through the swinging door.

The late bell rang.

In Gym, Mike was on my basketball team, and he played badly, as usual. But what was new was how hard he fired his passes. Like he didn't want you to catch it, he wanted to kill you with it. He threw the ball like a crazy person. That goon didn't know how lucky he was. Mike could've creamed him in two seconds flat.

He'd been doing aikido since sixth grade.

Chapter 4

I had early lunch, which mostly was a drag, since I usually wasn't that hungry at eleven-thirty in the morning. But on gym days I didn't mind so much.

Mike and I came into the cafeteria and grabbed a couple of red plastic trays and joined the line. Mike got grilled cheese. I got a burger and a cola, and a burger and lemonade and a large fries for B.J. They didn't have those chocolate donuts.

Toby James's mother usually worked the cash register, but that day it was another woman, a woman with piled yellow hair and no expression on her face. After we paid and were looking around for a table, Mike said, "So where's Toby's mother? Huh?"

I frowned. "Quit it, would you? You're making

me nuts. What do you think, Toby's mother got arrested too?"

"It's not possible?"

"I saw Toby in Trig. He didn't look especially worried about anything."

"Oh," said Mike. "Good."

And he laughed at himself, but he didn't laugh all that hard.

B.J. was eating her hamburger like some guy at a hockey game, just wolfing it down. On the table at her elbow was a notebook, and she had her math text standing up against a napkin dispenser. While she ate, she did homework, zipping through equations like they were nothing.

She was a lefty and wrote hook-handed. I'd always—or at least since I'd started liking B.J.—kind of wished I was left-handed too. I figured if I was a lefty, it'd be just one more thing we had in common. Our houses had the same color aluminum siding. Both our mothers were born in April, in the same year, 1953.

Mike picked at my coleslaw and kept frowning.

Until last month, there used to be music playing in the cafeteria during lunch. Then one day suddenly it wasn't playing anymore. Mr. Belton said it just made the whole atmosphere too "rowdy." Typically, Mike thought it was one more part of what the Government called the nation's Moral Renewal, and what he called the Big Crackdown. And maybe it was. Maybe it was.

I finished lunch and started looking around. I watched some dopey freshmen have a fish-patty fight, and then I watched a couple of teachers pay for their lunches. They carried their trays across the cafeteria and into the faculty lounge. The door was open, as usual, and I could see the coffee urn they had set up in there on a trestle table. Then Mr. Laudermilch stepped out of the lounge. Our eyes met and he smiled. I looked away, and when I looked back, he was talking to Will Farmer.

Mike said, "I'd like to drop that guy Farmer down a deep well." He was looking where I was looking, seeing what I was seeing. I smiled, but I felt anything but smiley inside.

I was remembering, again, just how tight Will and I once were. We'd known each other all our lives, practically. When we were little kids, his family lived across the street, and we used to play with action figures in our backyards. Will had some wild imagination and was always thinking up great stories for us to act out with those six-inch superheroes. We used to go hiking together, too. Pack lunches and jugs of Kool-Aid and walk out to the farms, which aren't even there anymore, then play hide-and-seek in the tomato fields.

He was smart, always. Once, for a fifth-grade science fair, he built a working lock, like in the Panama Canal. He built it out of Plexiglas and rubber tubing. That was the same year I'd put together an electromagnet that just wouldn't work.

And we used to go to the town library, at least twice a week. While I was still taking out picture books, he was already reading science books, geography books, biographies. I remember him reading about Thomas Edison, Theodore Roosevelt,

Harry Truman. Books in the Great Americans series. He loved those books and used to say, only semijoking, that he was going to be a Great American himself one day. I believed him. He was my best friend. Even when his family moved across town and he went to another grammar school, we stayed best friends and got together every weekend.

In high school, though, things started cooling between us. I hit it off with Mike Fromkin, and Will and Mike just never did, for some reason. Mike thought Will was a snob, but Mike had always been way too sensitive. He thought a lot of people were snobs who just weren't. But it wasn't only Mike that came between me and Will. There were other things, too.

As he got more and more popular, people started making demands on his time, and he liked that. He loved being the center of a group. I'd never been a group person. Not that I was a loner, I just preferred a small circle of close pals I could depend on.

Will became interested in politics, and by sophomore year, he was captain of the Debating Club. I went to a few of his debates, and he always demolished his opponents. He didn't believe in half the opinions he had to argue—he told me so himself—he just loved to argue, to score points, to see if he could find merit in different points of view. And of course, he also loved to win, to be the winner. I guess he still did.

* * *

"You know that little storefront on North Main," Mike was saying now, interrupting my thoughts, "where every time there's an election one of the candidates rents it for a campaign office? The storefront," he said, "next to Modern Yarn."

I realized he'd been talking for some time already, but I didn't know what about. I smiled, not wanting him to guess I hadn't been paying attention. "Yeah," I said, "what about it?"

"So who do I see strolling out of there yesterday but our friend Will Farmer. And he's lugging a bunch of cartons. How much you want to make a bet that's where they got all those flyers printed up? How much you want to make a bet the New Cops got another of their substations right in that store! Young Patriots," he grumbled. "That's no school club, if you want my opinion. They're just cheerleaders. Cheerleaders for the generals in Washington. Cheerleaders and snitches."

"Keep it down," said B.J. glancing sharply at Mike, her jawline hardening.

Keep it down, keep it down. That was the worst part of all this stuff, all the stuff that had happened since last January. The keep-it-down-keep-it-down business. People had been arrested, people—including the Mayor and the head of the local Chamber of Commerce—had disappeared, the newspapers had gotten thinner, the radio was a joke. But the worst part of it all for me, so far, was that at least once every day I heard somebody tell somebody else, "Keep it down." And I always got a stomach cramp, half-expecting to see another somebody standing there listening, another somebody with a rifle or a machine gun or something like that. Suddenly you felt you had to keep quiet about so many things. Keep it down, keep it down.

Chapter 5

After lunch I had History, and of course Mr. Kantrowitz didn't show. Laudermilch did.

Before the bell, he just stood up there in front of the room, in front of the laminated map of Europe, not saying a word. But if anybody opened his mouth, Laudermilch's head swiveled around with the speed of light and shot the kid a death ray. Finally, the bell rang and he rubbed his hands together. "Your regular teacher is not here," he said, and I thought that was sort of odd. Why didn't he mention Kantrowitz's name?

"So," he said, "you can use this class time for a study period." He smiled. But he was a big flop as a friendly guy. "However, before you begin to study—quietly—I'll collect your homework."

That did it. Then and there I decided that Mike

was right about this guy. Something was definitely off. No substitute ever collected homework.

As everybody was fishing out diskettes, Mr. Laudermilch zipped open his briefcase. Then with a phony snap of his fingers, trying to make us all believe he'd just thought of something, he said, "And I've been asked to collect your class texts, as well."

You could see the puzzled expressions on thirty faces, but nobody said a word.

I got out my diskette, made sure the name tape was still in place, and passed it forward. Then I took one last flip through our paperback history text, noticing some of the places in there that I'd highlighted with Magic Marker. A few passages in the chapter about Tom Paine, a whole paragraph in the chapter about Lenin, and a section in the chapter about de Gaulle. We still had a quarter of the book to get through before June, and I couldn't figure out how come they were being collected now. Were we going to get them back? I mean, it wasn't a workbook, it was a textbook, *Conflicts in a Changing World.*

I brought out my Trig homework, started doing some problems. And I sure wished that B.J. was there to help me. I was a borderline moron when it came to math, and my mind wandered. I got sleepy. I looked at Laudermilch seated behind his desk, doing absolutely nothing, except staring at his fingertips.

I thought about Kantrowitz, about how he'd pace back and forth when he lectured, about how he'd jab a finger into the air and laugh at his own corny jokes, and about how he used to say that we should be wary of any word with *ism* at the end of it: Communism, Fascism, even Americanism. Fanatics, he used to tell us, are all the same underneath. Had he really been arrested?

I looked out the window. The day had brightened some. It wasn't so cloudy, and the breeze had quit. In the branches of a big chestnut tree I saw more of those big sparrows, their heads twitching this way and that, that way and this.

Suddenly there was a loud rumbling sound, and the birds looked up. It was just another transport plane. You got used to them, living so close to an Air Force base. The rumbling passed, and then I was thinking about last January eighteenth, when all night long, all through the night and into the next morning, we kept hearing one plane right after another pass overhead.

I remembered how Mom kept wringing her hands and racing from room to room, throwing up the windows and looking out. She was in her bathrobe, and her hair was uncombed, and it got wilder and wilder looking because she kept pushing her fingers through it.

I remembered Dad finally telling her to relax, just relax, breathe deep, and I remembered that she started to cry, gulping for air. "It can't be," she was saying over and over, "it can't be. It can't be."

We'd had every radio and TV in the house turned on, each tuned to a different channel or station. But around two in the morning, every channel, every station suddenly had the same guy on, Colonel Somebody saying that the President of the United States had been relieved of his duties and that the Congress had been dismissed. He said everything was okay, everything was necessary and okay. The Joint Chiefs of Staff were now in charge. And nobody should panic.

Then the three of us just sat there like stone in front of the television set waiting for more news. Waiting, I think, for somebody to come on, maybe Johnny Carson, and say it was all a great big national joke, that it hadn't really happened.

But instead of Johnny Carson we got General James Gregory Sawchuk, at four A.M. All his brass shone in the television lights, and he dripped perspiration the whole time that he talked, but never once did he lift a finger to flick any from his upper lip. The General repeated what the spokesman had said earlier. Yes, the military had, in fact, taken charge of the government. Yes, the Congress had been relieved of its duties and responsibilities, and yes, President Cudahy was currently under arrest. But, he said, leaning forward, his mouth bending into the faintest smile, he felt that the country deserved a full explanation for all of these momentous events.

That's when the color maps started to appear, one right after the other, on a projection screen behind him. First Mexico, then Nicaragua, Saudi Arabia, Syria, Lebanon, Israel, Iraq, and Iran. And the General, biting his words off and speaking almost through clenched teeth, accused President Cudahy and his majority Neo-Liberal Party of ignoring political, strategic, and moral realities. "While the former president," he said, "was cutting defense budgets and canceling weapons-procurement programs, while he was endangering the ability of this nation to defend itself and to maintain our proper spheres of interest around the world, the enemies of America were laying the groundwork for Communist revolution in Mexico and for the ultimate triumph of anti-American fanaticism in the Middle East. Finally, with the governments of Mexico and Saudi Arabia on the brink of collapse, and with our most cherished values in the most serious jeopardy, the Joint Chiefs of Staff decided, by unanimous vote, that we could no longer stand by and see the United States destroyed by President Cudahy's weakness, indecision, and lack of moral will."

General Sawchuk leaned back in his seat, glanced to his left, nodded, then faced the cameras again. "The transfer of power tonight has been achieved without violence or bloodshed. We trust that public order can be similarly maintained."

That sounded like a threat to me.

He God-blessed us, then all television and radio reception turned to snow and static.

Mom couldn't stop crying. I got the shivers and maybe I started crying too. Dad tried to call one of his newspaper friends, but our phone was dead. The phones were dead all over America.

Chapter 6

Thursday and Friday, Kantrowitz wasn't in school again, but neither was Laudermilch. Instead, for History and Homeroom we had a regular substitute, a guy we've had before, named Simmons, who always wore the same boring blue suit. This was the first time, though, that he came in wearing a 119 pin. Like Laudermilch, he never mentioned Kantrowitz by name. He seemed kind of nervous, and when Michelle Nilan raised her hand and asked him when Mr. K would be back, he turned pale.

We got a brand-new history text, *American Power, Past and Present.*

At lunch Friday, Mike told me that Artie Ross said he'd seen two New Cops coming out of Mr. K's apartment house on Cleveland Street. But you just couldn't believe Artie Ross. Last month he'd said that the President had been shot by a firing squad—that he'd been marched out to the Lincoln Memorial. At dawn. Artie said he'd heard it on the radio. But that was a lie. The whole thing was a lie.

Every once in a while we'd see a picture in the paper of Patrick Cudahy at his Oregon ranch, puttering around or mending a fence or something. He didn't look happy, but he looked healthy enough. Supposedly, he supported the generals now. At least that's what it said in the photo captions. Anyway, he hadn't been shot. That was the whole point.

Mike had said a couple of times that it could be Cudahy's double we were seeing in all those photographs. The generals could've fixed up some guy with plastic surgery to resemble the President. I wished he wouldn't talk like that so much. He sounded like Mom. She had those kinds of theories, too. I worried about them both. You never knew who might get wind of what they'd been saying. Anybody could've been a snitch. The cafeteria ladies, the mailman, the gas-and-electric meter reader...

Chapter 7

Mike picked me up Friday night in his grandparents' car—a maroon Pontiac Triton with almost ninety thousand miles on the odometer—and as usual I had to dump soda cans and pretzel bags and a bunch of his little brother's comic books off the passenger seat before I could even sit down.

On the drive over to get B.J., Mike asked me if I remembered his Uncle Art who lived downstate, and I said yeah, picturing a thin, nervous guy, about thirty, who wore thick, bottle-bottom glasses. "Yeah, I remember him," I said. "What about him?"

"He called my grandmother this afternoon. And guess what? There's going to be a big demonstration Sunday at the University of Dayton."

"What kind of demonstration?"

"Against what's happened, of course. Harry Thomas is going to be there, supposedly."

"Yeah?"

Popular guy, Harry Thomas. He used to be an astronaut before he got elected to Congress about fifteen years ago. Ran for president once, when I was ten. Mom and Dad voted for him, and Mom, especially, thought he was Mr. Wonderful. He wasn't a senator anymore. But then nobody was a senator anymore.

"You want to drive down?" Mike asked me.

"Where? To Dayton? Are you crazy?"

"I'm not crazy, no."

"Just forget it, Mike, okay?"

He pressed his lips together.

"You're real brave," I said. "You'll go to some demonstration where maybe you'll get gassed, but you won't ask Monica Lando for a date. Or Jill Sullivan."

It was dark in the car, but I would've bet ten bucks that he blushed.

"I don't like Monica Lando," he said. "And Jill Sullivan only goes out with blond guys."

"So ask somebody else."

"I thought we were talking about Dayton," he said.

"I changed the subject."

At B.J.'s, her mother answered the door and smiled me inside. She seemed a little unsteady on her feet, and she slurred a little, but I tried not to notice.

"I'll go tell Betty Jean you're here," she said.

Only her parents called her Betty Jean. B.J. hated the name herself. Thought it made her sound like a waitress at a truck stop, or a has-been country-and-western singer.

Mrs. Pendleton left me in the parlor and I sat down. On the coffee table, next to a full ashtray and a half-full glass of white wine, was a stack of magazines. I picked one up, a thick square thing with a plain boring cover. One of Mr. Pendleton's scientific journals.

He wasn't home, of course.

He hardly ever was, these days.

I'd known B.J.'s father for years, been over his house probably hundreds of times, but the only time that I'd ever heard him talk about his work—he did "research and development" at Harris Air Force Base—was at a barbecue that past July.

The summer of 1994 had been bad news. One day you'd hear about all the fighting down in Mexico City between the government and the guerrilla army. Next day, you'd hear about the joint American and Russian expeditionary force landing troops in Iran. A hairy time. And I couldn't make heads or tails of what was going on, really. But I knew enough to know that things were dangerous all over. People in Sandersville were walking around with worried faces, and their tempers were short.

While all of that was happening, the Pendletons decided to have a barbecue. Which was a little weird, but so what. Like Dad was always saying, life goes on.

B.J. invited me and I went, but I hardly knew any of the people. They were mostly friends of

Mr. Pendleton's from the base. A few of them were Air Force, but they weren't dressed in uniforms or anything.

I volunteered to cook the burgers, and, since there were at least twenty-five guests, that kept me busy all afternoon. I'd cook, and B.J. would hold the buns open for the hot dogs and hamburgers, then take a plate of them to the picnic tables.

About seven o'clock, Mr. Pendleton came over. B.J. had gone into the house to make coffee. Her mother had had too many gin-and-tonics and was lying down. I'd about finished grilling burgers, and in fact that's what Mr. Pendleton wanted to talk to me about, to thank me for helping out. From the way he was rocking on his heels, I could tell he was a bit tipsy. He wasn't polluted or anything, just tipsy. There was a blob of catsup on his sport shirt. He put a hand on my shoulder and stuck his big face close to mine. I smelled india relish, mustard, and beer on his breath. He asked me how I'd been, and I told him okay, considering. And he asked me, "Considering what?"

I shrugged and said, "Well, you know. All this stuff we're always hearing about. Like, there's going to be a revolution in Mexico, a war here, another war there. It's starting to look like I'm either gonna be a soldier or a cinder by this time next year."

"Listen," he said, dropping into a whisper and clapping an arm across my back, "when I was your age, even younger, we had the Cuban Missile Crisis. Heard of that?"

My mother had mentioned it herself recently, several times. Sure I'd heard of it, but I wasn't too clear about what had actually happened. Kennedy was president—right? I knew that much.

"We all thought we were going to die," said Mr. Pendleton, slurring a little. "I was a boy and I thought it was the end of the world. And here we are, thirty-two years later. The world didn't end, did it?"

I smiled.

"Nothing too serious is going to happen, Eddie. Don't you worry." He lowered his voice again, and his lips tightened into an arrogant smile. "Because the Soviets know and the Mexicans know and the Saudis know, and every single other one of those bastards knows that all across America there are people who've been working their tails off to make sure this country is the strongest one on earth. People like me. People like them." He swept an arm to indicate his guests. "Thank God there's people like us. Thank God there's laboratories like ours—eh?"

For some reason, that chilled me. But I managed to smile anyway.

"Don't worry, Eddie," he finished, squeezing my shoulder. "Don't you worry. We've got the smarts, Eddie. We've got the weapons. Nobody's going to mess." Then all of a sudden, his face darkened and his voice took on an edge, and he said, "Unless, of course, that wimp we have for a president keeps cutting back on defense spending."

Then B.J. returned, and when she saw the two

of us standing there nose to nose in the twilight, she laughed. "What on earth are you two birds talking about?" she asked.

Mr. Pendleton winked at me and put a finger to his lips. He winked again...

"Hi, Eddie!"

It was B.J., at last. She came into the parlor wearing cola-colored jeans and a yellow jersey. She had on some makeup, not much but some, and her hair was brushed silky. It bounced as she moved. She looked nice.

"Ready?" I asked her.

Mrs. Pendleton asked us where we were going, and I said I guessed the movies, though I hadn't checked what was playing. She told B.J. midnight, then gave her a peck on the cheek and we left.

"Is Mike with us?" B.J. asked on our way down the front steps.

I rolled my eyes. "Sure is," I said. "We're even taking his car tonight. You really got to fix him up with somebody."

"Forget it," said B.J. "He's too choosy."

"He's not. He's too chicken."

We rode downtown and parked in the free lot behind Beimdeck's Drugs, then walked along South Main to the Victory Theatre. It was about ten of eight, and a bunch of kids I knew from school were standing outside looking at the posters.

A Stu Haring picture was playing, something called *Last Deceit.* Mike said he'd heard it was a thriller, a murder mystery. B.J. loved Stu Haring and I liked him well enough, so we decided to give it a try.

But the picture was bad, incredibly dumb. It was a murder mystery, all right—Stu Haring played a race-car mechanic whose girlfriend was being stalked by a hired killer—but it didn't make any sense. It was a big jumble, and besides that, it was short, only about an hour and fifteen minutes.

When the lights came on, you could hear people all around the theater saying things like "What happened?" "I don't get it." "Did you understand it?" Generally, everybody agreed you couldn't make any sense of the story.

As I was walking up the aisle with B.J. and Mike, though, I overheard some guy say to his wife that he'd seen the same picture last month in Toronto and that it had been a whole lot longer. "They cut a bunch of scenes," he said, but when he noticed me eavesdropping, his cheeks reddened, and he reached for his jacket. I wondered what those scenes were about, and felt like asking, but finally I didn't.

It was still early when we came out, so we decided to walk over to the Colony Diner for something to eat. There was a real crush at the door, though, and we had to stand in the vestibule and wait for a booth. We were still waiting ten minutes later when two New Cops in black leather uniforms showed up. They shouldered past everybody and went straight inside.

The hostess was a short dumpy redhead called Sugar, and Sugar immediately walked up to them and apologized for the delay. They didn't even look at her. They just stood on their toes and scanned the diner, then ambled like hotshot motorcycle boys over to a corner table that hadn't yet been cleared of plates. Sugar pressed her lips together angrily, but then snapped her fingers at a busboy and told him to clear the table for the NCs. I heard Mike sigh noisily.

Finally, Sugar signaled that our booth was ready. We scooted over to where she pointed, slid in, and a waitress promptly brought us three gigantic laminated menus. We ordered three coffees and three reubens.

There was a table juke fastened to the wall, and while we were waiting for the food, B.J. flipped through it, seeing what songs were available. More than half the selection tabs were empty. We all knew why that was.

Thank you, General Sawchuk. And up yours.

Our sandwiches came, and while we were eating, a tall, slim, curly-haired guy, maybe twenty-five, but maybe not even, strolled into the diner. He was wearing old jeans and a faded denim jacket that was studded with buttons that all said No, with double exclamation points. In his left ear he had a tiny gold earring.

He stood by the cashier's station, just scoping the place and everybody in it.

A few minutes later I looked for him again, and he was sitting on a stool with his back to the counter. A mug of black coffee stood by his elbow and a cigarette was smoking between his fingers. He rubbed out the cigarette, then reached a hand into his jacket, and when he took it out again, he was holding a stiff, dead sparrow. Which he casually tossed, like it was a book of matches or a set of keys. It fell with a dull smack on the New Cops' table. Then in a loud voice, loud enough that everybody in the diner flinched, he said, "This isn't one of yours, is it?"

The cops gaped at the Denim Guy like he was a blue and orange Martian, and he just grinned back at them. Then, moving slowly, their leather squeaking, they got up from their table. The Denim Guy slid off his stool. I glanced at B.J. for a split second—that's all—but when I looked back, one of the cops was doubled over and grunting. Then he pitched forward and hit the floor, his legs sprawled toward our booth. The second cop tried to unsnap his gun holster, but the Denim Guy dropped him with a chop to the side of the head. Start to finish, it had taken maybe ten seconds, and both cops were out cold.

The diner turned as quiet as a church before a funeral. Everybody stared at the Denim Guy, who spread his hands, shrugged innocently, then stooped down, frisked one of the cops, and unclipped something from his garrison belt. Something that looked kind of like a telephone beeper. He stuck that into his pocket, nodded at everybody, then left, in no special hurry.

Chapter 8

Sandersville was a great town to be a little kid in. The problem was, it wasn't so great when you got older. Same old story. No place, really, to go. Small houses, medium-size houses, schools and churches, one shopping street, one movie, one diner. There used to be a bowling alley, but it went out of business. There were a couple of parks, but they closed after sundown.

So, even though it wasn't curfew yet, B.J., Mike and me were strapped for something to do. Finally we decided just to call it a night. Other Fridays we'd driven around, talking and laughing, but after what happened at the diner, we were all feeling shaky.

Mike cruised down Truman Street and pulled over to the curb. B.J. and I slid out, then I walked around to the driver's window and bent down. "Call you tomorrow, Mike."

"You want me to wait?"

"No."

"Sure, okay." He looked a little disappointed, and it ticked me off, some. I felt like telling him, Get your own girl. But I didn't. I stood back and he drove off.

Going up B.J.'s walk, I noticed the garage doors were open about a third of the way and that yellow light was spilling out from underneath onto the driveway, onto the hood and fender of the Pendletons' new Buick.

Mr. Pendleton used the garage for his workshop.

As soon as we went in the house, B.J. started whispering, and I did the same thing. Her mom was one of those people who went to bed at ten o'clock every night, no matter what. Monday night, Friday night, it was all the same to her.

"You want a cup of coffee?" B.J. asked, and I said no, thanks. So we just tossed our jackets over a chair in the parlor and sat down.

Right away, B.J. picked up the remote and ran through all the broadcast and cable stations. There were a bunch of old movies on, some of them really, really old—one of them was a Jimmy Cagney picture—but nothing that we felt like watching. Me, I would've turned the TV off, but B.J. left it on with the volume down. Jimmy Cagney was dancing across a stage in a straw hat and a striped jacket.

I looked at B.J. and cleared my throat, then didn't know what I wanted to say, or if I wanted to say anything. She was looking at me with a weak half smile.

I really liked her, you know? I liked her enough that lately I'd found myself thinking about us two years from now, five years from now. About us being at the same college together, away from home. That always got me a little dizzy, thinking about that. Thinking about what it'd be like to spend as much time together as we pleased, whenever we pleased, wherever.

I was afraid to tell her about all those thoughts of mine, though. I was afraid of how she might take the news.

Anyway, after sitting in her parlor for maybe five minutes, I started to feel antsy, a little desperate to say something, anything, so I said, "Maybe if the weather stays nice, we could go out to Panther Lake next weekend."

She nodded, but I knew she wasn't listening. Then she turned, hands clenched in her lap, and looked at me intently. Her lips were a tight line. "That guy was something, wasn't he? I didn't even see what he did to that first cop—did you, Eddie?"

"No," I told her, and my gut tightened and I recognized the stupid feeling, the stupid jealous feeling, and without realizing what I was doing, I leaned over and kissed B.J. It was an awkward kiss. She'd been in the process of turning her head, so I ended up kissing her on the jaw. She laughed. I almost did. Then we fell silent again.

On the TV, Jimmy Cagney was dancing down a carpeted staircase.

"I think I'd better get going," I said.

B.J. didn't ask me to stay. That was discouraging.

I threw on my jacket and she walked me to the front door.

It was pretty cold outside, so cold that I saw my breath blow off as vapor. I stuck my hands into my pockets and went down the steps.

Mr. Pendleton startled me.

He was standing in the driveway and smoking a cigarette. He had one foot up on the bumper of his car. Behind him, the garage door was all the way up.

I startled him, too.

"Oh—Eddie," he said. "How's it going?"

"All right. How are you, Mr. Pendleton?"

He didn't reply. All he did was remove his foot from the Buick and toss his cigarette onto the hardtop. Then he ground out the coal with his heel. "It must be thirty-five degrees," he said, with a little laugh. "May in the Midwest!" His face was lit by the garage light, and he looked—well, he looked old. And I knew for a fact that he was four years younger than my own father. He looked tired and he looked sad. He looked worried.

"How's school, Eddie?" He'd turned away from me and was facing the front lawn, and I got the impression that he wasn't talking to me, really, that he was just talking. Just talking, making sounds.

"School's all right," I said.

"Good," he said flatly. "Good." Then he sighed. "Must be wonderful being seventeen."

I said I guessed so.

Then he blinked and came out of his trance. "Good night, Eddie," he said, and turned to walk back into the garage.

And that's when I noticed the stuff lying scattered on top of the workbench inside. Microchips and wires, circuitry, transistors, and film canisters. And birds, all in pieces. Wings here, heads there. What must have been half a dozen sparrows, made out of plastic.

Chapter 9

Because Dad was still away, I helped Mom do the grocery shopping that Saturday morning. We left around ten to drive to Freedom Plaza, the big mall on Route 9, a couple miles from town. We took the Beast—what we called Mom's '89 Chevy station wagon—and it kept bucking and backfiring, and once it even stalled.

While I drove, Mom checked over the shopping list and fetched out an envelope full of coupons. Coupons for catsup, soap, coffee, orange juice, and paper towels, coupons for practically everything. As usual, I teased her about them. She'd spend whole evenings just clipping them out of newspapers and magazines. "I save ten dollars a week using these stupid things," she said and laughed, and I glanced at her, and it was great to see a smile on her face. I can't tell you how great it was. I hadn't seen one in a couple of weeks.

The mall was crowded, and I had to park a good distance from Kroger's. I grabbed a shopping cart that somebody had left by a vapor lamp and pushed that as Mom trotted alongside me past a movie-rental and a pizza parlor, a liquor store, a pet shop, and a little card-and-gift.

It was outside the card shop that I saw Mr. Laudermilch, who'd subbed that first day Mr. Kantrowitz hadn't shown up at school. He was speaking to a blond-haired woman, who was about fifty.

The pair of them were dressed in military uniforms.

I guess my mouth dropped open, because Mom looked at me and asked, "What's wrong?"

"Nothing," I said. By then Laudermilch was behind us, and he hadn't recognized me. I looked back. He and the woman were strolling off. He was carrying a greeting-card bag with a paisley design on it, and she was unwrapping the cellophane from a package of tiny cigars.

"Why are you so interested in those two?" Mom asked me.

"I'm not interested," I said.

"Have you seen them before? If you've seen them before, Eddie, that could mean something. Tell me!"

She was all tensed, her eyes open wide. She'd gone pale, was getting manic again, and suddenly

I was afraid for her. "Come on, Mom, relax," I said, "would you?"

I wheeled the cart through Kroger's and Mom loaded it. Toothpaste, tissues, powdered donuts, chicken cutlets, iceberg lettuce, cans of soup. And every time she got something that she had a coupon for, she took the coupon from her envelope and stuck it into her jacket pocket. She was an organized shopper. She had a system.

We came to the coffee and tea aisle, and while she was searching the shelves for a particular brand of decaf, an older man came by carrying a plastic basket filled with frozen TV dinners and a six-pack of Mounds bars. He had a brush-cut and a small, trim mustache, and he was dressed in an enlisted man's uniform. He stood patiently behind Mom, and she was so preoccupied with looking that she didn't realize he was there. Finally she turned around and bumped right into him. Startled, she dropped her two-pound can of Maxwell House.

The soldier apologized, stooping to pick up the coffee.

I saw Mom glance at him, and then she was moving away, heading quickly down the aisle. The man, still in a crouch, called after her, "Lady, your coffee!" He looked at me with a baffled expression. I took the can and tossed it in my cart.

I found Mom two aisles away, standing next to a display of Saltine crackers. She was trembling. When she saw me, she blinked several times as though just waking up from a deep sleep, a troubling dream. But then she gave a little laugh and rolled her eyes, mocking herself. "Let's finish and get out of here, okay?"

But we never did finish. What happened was, we kept seeing that soldier from the coffee aisle, which was natural enough, but each time we passed him, Mom would clench her hands and move rapidly away, almost running.

Finally, in the dairy aisle, she said, "He's following us."

"Mom."

"Eddie, he's following us. I know it."

"He's just a guy."

"No, he's following us. Who is he? Tell me, Eddie!" Her voice was shaking.

"How should I know who he is?"

"Come on, Eddie, tell me. The way you looked at him outside—you know who he is."

"Mom, that's not the guy I saw outside. What're you talking about? It's a different guy—Mom?"

I was feeling sick to my stomach.

"Eddie, we have to go."

"All right, let's pay for this stuff and go. Fine," I said, feeling sicker.

But she wanted to leave the groceries. I told her that was dumb, but she didn't care, she wasn't listening. She kept looking around for the soldier with the short gray hair.

"I want to leave right now!" she said. "I don't see him! It's a good time."

I said all right. I guess I wanted to get out of there too. I wanted to get Mom out. So we abandoned the cart in the dairy aisle and simply left. Mom kept looking straight ahead, and she was breathing like she'd just come up from being held under water. I saw the soldier she was so afraid of at a checkout counter, picking down a copy of *TV Guide* from the rack.

He didn't notice us when we went by. I don't think.

Chapter 10

Dad had promised to be home by noon on Sunday, but the afternoon passed and he never came. Never called, either. I was worried, but you should've seen Mom. She was a wreck.

Around six o'clock, Mike Fromkin dropped over with his kid brother, Sammy, who was nine and a third-grader at Glenn Elementary.

Mike did that a lot, just came by when I wasn't expecting him. Usually I didn't mind. That day, though, I wasn't in much of a mood to hang out, which was what Mike wanted to do.

"What's the matter?" he asked me, giving me a frown, since I'd given him one.

"Nothing."

"You eating dinner or something?" Sammy asked.

I shook my head.

"Good," said Mike, and he dipped a hand into his jacket pocket and pulled out two unlabeled audiotapes. He shook them happily in my face and said, "The newest Ricky Boys and—ta-dum! the latest Sunday Orphans, all sixteen songs!"

"No kidding," I said, sort of interested even if I was still in a funk. "Where'd you get those?"

"From Richie Vorius," said Sammy, and immediately Mike gave him a shove.

"Listen, stupid, this is Eddie and it's okay to say anything, but maybe you're too quick to give answers, huh?"

"What're you talking about?" said Sammy, rubbing his shoulder. "Next time you try that, jerk, you're gonna get a black eye."

"Right. From who?" Mike turned back to me and lifted his eyebrows. "I got 'em from Richie, yeah," he said. Since the Bazaar had left town, Richie was the guy to see if you wanted banned records or tapes. "So, you feel like listening?"

"Yeah, all right," I said, and as I was walking Mike and Sammy up to my room, Mom came in through the kitchen from the backyard. Mike called out a friendly hello, which she didn't seem to hear. It wasn't Dad, Dad wasn't home, and that's all that counted. She said something under her breath, then turned and walked away.

"Maybe we should leave," Sammy told Mike.

"No," I said, "don't. It's all right."

"Maybe we should," Mike said. "Is she mad or something?"

"No, just forget it." I shrugged. "My father's late." Then without thinking, I said, "I hope he didn't have an accident." Which was a stupid thing to mention because that's how Mike's and Sammy's father—and mother—died. In a seven-car smashup on the Ohio Pike, near Bowling Green. Four years ago.

Mike tossed one of the cassettes on my bed, then kicked off his running shoes. Sammy immediately started to snoop, looking at the trophies and junk on my wall shelves, squatting to check out the books in my bookcase. I popped the tape into the deck.

"Crank it up," said Mike.

"That's not a great idea."

"Oh yeah. Your mom. I forgot. How late is he?"

"About six hours."

"Where's he been?"

"A few places."

"What's he taking pictures of this time?"

"A power plant," I said. "And then he was doing a lot of junk for *People* magazine. A woman in a wheelchair who paints with her teeth, or something."

Sammy laughed, and Mike said, "You're a jerk."

"Look who's talking!" Sammy had pulled a couple of paperback novels out of the bookcase and was flipping through them. I got the impression he was looking for pictures, and was disappointed. He probably would've liked one of Mom's books, but I didn't keep those out. I stashed them in my drawer. Because I wanted them to stay in mint condition, not for any other reason.

The Sunday Orphans was a pretty good band, but not one of my favorites. I didn't even know much about them, whether they were English, Australian, American, Japanese, or what. You couldn't find any rock magazines on the newsstands anymore. Last time I'd seen *Rolling Stone* or *Spin* or *Crash* was back in March. So I didn't know much about the Orphans, or like them much, but I gave the tape a closer listen than I might've if they hadn't been on the X-list. I tried listening to the lyrics, but there was nothing I could pick out that seemed especially political or obscene. Maybe I missed the whole point, but to me the songs sounded like the same old boy-girl stuff, with a whole lot of synth and found-noise.

Mike listened with his eyes shut—he always listened to music like that. I sat in a chair and stared off into space.

"This music stinks," said Sammy.

Mike cocked one eye open to glare at his kid brother, then resumed his meditations.

"Eddie. You want to know what Mike paid for this junky tape? You want me to tell you?"

"Shut up, jerk," said Mike, this time not even bothering to open an eye.

Sammy shrugged. He was sitting like an Indian on my rug, pulling all sorts of stuff out of his jeans: a tiny rubber action figure (Grogar the Terrible), a couple of crumpled-up M&M bags, and several paint-dappled stones. Since he was five or six, he'd been collecting rocks and stones, which he'd dribbled and speckled with phosphorescent paint. He claimed he could do magic with them, depending upon how he arranged the stones, in a mound, a circle, a semicircle, or whatever. Kind of a flaky kid.

Now he made a circle with them on my rug. He flattened out the candy bags in the center of it, and finally pulled something from his shirt that made me sit up straight.

"Where'd you get that?"

"Hey," said Mike, "you guys mind not talking? I'm trying to listen, here."

"I got it over by the reservoir," said Sammy, ignoring his brother.

I went and joined Sammy on the floor.

"It's a circle of power," he explained, pointing at his construction. "You know anything about circles of power?"

"No, nothing," I said, then reached into the circle.

"Hey, Eddie, don't!" He knocked my hand away. "You can't just do that. That's major energy there. You want to burn your fingers? That's a circle of power!"

"Circle of stupidity," Mike jeered, rolling onto his side to see what the heck was going on.

"Okay, I won't touch," I told Sammy. "But what's that thing there in the center?"

Sammy moved his shoulders in a half shrug. "I told you already, I found it over by the reservoir. It's some toy, I guess. What's it look like?"

What it looked like, and what it was, was a sparrow's head with a lot of electronic circuitry sticking out the end.

Sammy deposited one final item—an empty raisin box—into the circle, then tightly squeezed his eyes shut. He grinned and clapped his hands. "That's that," he said, beginning to collect his stuff. "I just wiped out Hawaii with a tidal wave."

"Jerk," said Mike.

Sammy scooped up the sparrow's head and stuck it away in his pocket.

By ten of seven, I'd gotten so anxious about Dad that I just couldn't sit around anymore. Especially when the music wasn't so great. I was fidgeting and pacing, and finally I said, "Don't be ticked off or anything, okay? But I'm going to ask you guys to leave. And I'll see you tomorrow."

Sammy hopped to his feet. "We're being kicked out, Mike, come on." You could tell how much it was breaking his heart. He already had his hand on the doorknob.

I walked them downstairs and waved as they slumped off together. The same gait, the same hunch to their narrow shoulders. I couldn't hear what they were saying, but it looked like they were bickering again. At the corner, Sammy gave Mike a punch in the arm. Some things never changed. But some things did. I went back in the house.

Chapter 11

Dad got home after eleven.

As soon as his Ford pulled into the driveway, Mom and I both ran out. Dan smiled tiredly and ignored Mom's frantic questions. In fact, I don't think he spoke a word except hello till he was in the house and had tossed all his cameras on the sofa. Then he sat down, took a long, slow breath, and put his face in his hands.

That's when I saw that a clump of hair above his left ear was sticky and matted with blood.

Mom saw it too and let out a groan.

"It's okay, it's okay," Dad said, "I'm fine, just relax." He kept shaking his head, kept hushing Mom, kept tossing funny looks at me. But I didn't know what they meant, those looks.

"Who hurt you, Jerry?" Mom asked, about five times. "Where were you?"

Instead of answering, though, Dad just asked his own question. "Did you have the TV or the radio on today?"

"For a while," Mom answered. "Why? What's happened?" She was pale, and her hands were squeezed into fists.

Dad's brows raised and he let out a funny little laugh. "There wasn't anything about it on the TV? Nothing?"

"Nothing about what?" Mom was moving past fear into anger, quick. I could tell.

He looked around, his eyes picking up the drapes, the coffee table, the bookcase, but he wouldn't look at us. Then his eyes narrowed. "I want to show you both something," he said, then he picked up his cameras and we followed him downstairs to the basement, to his darkroom. He switched on a red light, poured chemicals into a tray, calibrated something on the developer, then told us, "I first heard about the demonstration last Tuesday."

"What demonstration?" Mom asked.

"In Dayton," Dad replied, and as soon as he did, my stomach felt like it was being squeezed. I remembered Mike talking about it, even asking me if I wanted to go.

Dad tugged a pair of rubber gloves on and plunged both hands into the chemical bath. "A big anti-Government rally down at the University of Dayton. Set for Sunday, today. Naturally, no permits were given out, and the Government and the university administration warned everybody not to show up. On Tuesday, I had no idea whether it would happen or not." He snapped on another red light. "Everyplace I went this entire week, Wednesday in Detroit, Thursday and Friday in Phoenix, I kept hearing things about the rally. It seemed to be getting bigger and bigger. Everybody knew about it."

"I didn't," said Mom.

I almost said that I did, but decided not to. I just stood and listened. I didn't breathe much.

"You called on Thursday," Mom said. "You didn't tell me anything about going to any demonstration."

"I wasn't planning to, I swear."

"And you shouldn't have, Jerry, you—"

"Do you want to hear what happened or not?"

"We want to hear, Dad," I said.

He looked at me, then moved his shoulders. "Yesterday," he said, "I was pretty much finished with my work." He snorted. "Spent a couple of wonderful hours with that snot Stu Haring. The movie star. Eddie, you must know who he is. What a creep! Lives right outside of Phoenix, him and his equally charming wife, the so-called singer. Twenty-year-old millionaire brats. Delightful assignments I've been getting lately."

Mom said, "Jerry . . ."

"Okay. I finished up with Haring and called an old buddy of mine I hadn't seen in five years. Jim McTague. Caught him just as he was packing, but he said sure, it'd be good to get together, and we met at a restaurant."

Dad stopped talking to stare at several of the prints which were just beginning to clarify in the developing fluid. I looked and saw Stu Haring's face emerge. Stu Haring leaning against a wooden corral. Stu Haring with his arm around the waist of his blond wife. Stu Haring buckling a saddle on a sleek chestnut mare. Dad rinsed off the prints and hung them up to dry.

"At first when I asked Jim where he was going on the trip, he kind of slid around it. Avoided giving me a straight answer. I got the impression he wasn't sure if he could trust me. And that bothered me. Anyway, I guess he finally decided to take a risk. Because he asked me if I'd heard anything about the demonstration in Dayton. I said sure, and he said, well, that's where he was going. He wasn't being sent by his paper. In fact, he'd be in deep trouble if they ever found out. Nobody was supposed to cover it. But Jimmy was going because—because he's a newsman." Dad paused, then shrugged. "To make a long story short, he asked me if I wanted to go to Dayton with him."

"And you said yes," Mom said.

Dad nodded. "Jimmy figured the major highways might have roadblocks. So we avoided them, kept to secondary roads, even back roads, and we traveled at night. Got to Dayton by eleven this morning.

"We parked about five miles from the university and started to hike. There were thousands of people, and everybody was in high spirits since there weren't any troops around. That was encouraging, but a little weird, too. Unbelievable. I mean, where was the Army? Where were the New Cops?

"By noon, there were maybe ten or fifteen thousand demonstrators on campus. And the only authorities any of us saw were the university police. And they stood back, left everybody alone. That's when I started taking pictures. Jimmy did too, and everybody kind of relaxed. Maybe the Government was backing down. Maybe this was the beginning of something. Maybe.

"Harry Thomas, Senator Thomas, got up and spoke, demanding that the Joint Chiefs call back Cudahy and the full Senate to Washington. He said that Cudahy had been right not to send military aid to the Mexican government, since it was corrupt and repressive and since the opposition had never been Marxist, contrary to what General Sawchuk claims. Good speech. Went on for maybe half an hour. He said that Cudahy made his fatal mistake last year when he agreed to send American troops to join the Russians in the Middle East. It didn't stabilize the region, and only gave people like Sawchuk too much clout in making foreign policy." Dad pulled another series of prints from the bath, clipped them up, tapped the edge of one with his index finger. "Then, around one o'clock, just after Senator Thomas finished talking, the birds came."

I looked at the prints and jerked reflexively. They all showed the same big, panicky crowd, and the crowd was running every which way. People were stumbling, some were even sprawled on the grass, being trampled. And the sky was dark with sparrows. I saw a bloodstain on the back of somebody's safari jacket. And I thought, I have a jacket just like that.

"I don't know what they are," Dad said in a choked voice. "And I don't know where the hell they came from. But they came." He shook his head. "Red eyes. They had red eyes. They attacked and they wouldn't stop. It was . . ." His voice trailed off.

Quietly, Mom said, "They attacked—I don't understand. Birds?"

"They're not alive, not real. Real birds don't explode on contact with human flesh."

Mom leaned against the wall and put a hand to her mouth, murmuring "Dear God, God . . ."

After that, Dad wouldn't, or couldn't, talk about it anymore. He said he was tired, exhausted, needed to go to bed. Putting her arm around his shoulders, Mom walked him up. I stayed behind and kept looking at the pictures on Dad's dryer line, and at one picture especially. That showed fifteen or twenty people sprinting like crazy over a grassy lawn, four tall dorm buildings in the background. I stared at those buildings, at the demonstrators running, and at the birds diving, swooping down.

I stared till my eyes watered. I guess I couldn't believe it.

Couldn't believe that it wasn't a movie still.

Chapter 12

B.J., Mike, and I had finished lunch and were hanging out in the quadrangle behind the school cafeteria. It was a Thursday afternoon, several weeks after the Dayton demonstration. The weather had turned nice, the trees were green, the flies were back.

We were talking, mostly about our plans for the summer. Mike had lined up a job at Kroger's—cashier, nine dollars an hour—and B.J. thought her father could find her clerical work at the base. That's what he'd promised her, at least, but so far he hadn't pulled any strings.

I didn't know what I was going to do all summer, and I said so.

"Well," said B.J., "maybe I can ask Dad to find you something, too." I could tell she thought that'd be real neat, us working at the base together. And

I guess I thought so, too. But? But it was just that—well, I didn't want to accept any favors from Mr. Pendleton.

I felt crummy about it, but lately whenever B.J. mentioned her father, I froze up inside and my teeth automatically clenched. She'd say something about Mr. Pendleton and I'd think of those birds, and blame him. I couldn't help it. I'd think of what Dad had told me about Dayton, and I'd remember the photographs that he'd developed, and I'd blame Mr. Pendleton. If that's how he made his living, building those things, then I didn't want anything to do with him. Period.

Mike stabbed a straw through the hole in an aseptic box of grape juice, then looked around and grimaced because Will Farmer had just come out of the cafeteria and was standing on the white-washed steps.

"General Farmer," Mike muttered.

Will's eyes roved around, taking everything in. He waved to a few kids, and most of them waved back. Not all of them. He used to be the most popular kid in the high school, but no longer. People still smiled at him, sure, but except for the Patriots, everybody kind of kept out of his way.

He came down the steps and started across the grassy quad, toward us. Then somebody called his name, in anger.

It was Richie Vorius.

"Trouble," said Mike, getting to his feet.

Richie was big and tough and more than a little dumb, a weightlifter with arms the size of deli hams, and the first thing that he did was shove

Will, hard, and send him staggering. Then, before Will could react, Richie straight-armed him again, and Will tripped over his own two feet and sprawled.

"I been meaning to talk to you, Farmer," said Richie.

"You got a funny way of talking," said Will, still on his butt.

"And you got a funny way of talking, too. Sounds to me more like squealing. When you talk, you sound more like a pig than a person. That's a fact."

Will didn't say anything.

"It was you, wasn't it?"

"What was?"

"Don't give me that, you Nazi scuz!"

Mike had walked up behind Richie, and he said something now, in a low voice. Richie responded by shaking his head from side to side. "Stay out of this, Fromkin. I mcan it. Me and this Nazi have something to settle."

"I'd watch your terminology, Richard," said Will, but still he wasn't getting up.

"My terminology," Richie said, his lips turning cruel, mocking. "You're so smart, Farmer. Big words, big man! Get up! You won't do anything without your bodyguards around to protect you, huh? I spent two days in jail on account of you!"

"Not on account of me," said Will.

"Bull! You told the cops that I sold records, didn't you? Didn't you! Admit it, creep, or I'll kick you where you are. Don't think I won't."

Then Mike stepped in front of Richie, saying,

"Lay off. You're not going to kick him. I'm not going to let you."

"You? You his friend or something?"

"No," Mike said quickly. "I'm not. But I'm yours."

"He told the cops—I know it was him. Everybody knows it was him, him and his Patriots." He made the word sound like it was spelled with only four letters. "It was him."

"Maybe, but if you do anything, Rich, I'll lay you out flat. And you know I can."

Richie stood there making and unmaking fists. But finally he turned away, then swaggered across the quad.

"You can get up now, Farmer," said Mike.

And slowly Will did, his bottom lip quivering. Maybe in humiliation, maybe in rage. I couldn't tell. I didn't know him anymore.

"Next time, Fromkin," he said, glaring, "just mind you own freakin' business."

We watched him walk slowly back into the cafeteria. And even though I knew that I shouldn't, I felt sorry for him.

Mike made a fist and banged himself with it, against his hip.

Chapter 13

Later that same afternoon, about two o'clock, B.J., Mike, and I—the Three Musketeers—along with the rest of the school, were sitting on bleachers in the gym. It was Senior Day, and the graduating class was going to put on some skits. But they were late getting started. Across the gym floor, on the opposite bleachers, the freshmen and sophomores were acting like real idiots, hooting and shrieking and stamping their feet. Somebody blew a horn. A length of pink toilet paper fluttered down from the top.

Finally Mr. Belton, the principal, took the stage. He started tapping the microphone and calling for attention. I saw one of the ceiling lights reflect off his 119 lapel button.

He welcomed us all to the Senior Theatrical, promised everybody a good time, then warned us that no nonsense would be tolerated. Typical. Make you feel good, then bum you right out.

At last, the skits began. They were pretty much the same ones as last year, a lot of silly junk, full of in-jokes and wisecracks about different teachers. Nobody made fun of Mr. Belton or Mr. Graham, or even mentioned Mr. Kantrowitz. Last year, I remembered, there'd been a skit where somebody acted the part of Mr. Kantrowitz, then lectured about the American Revolution while he ate one glazed donut after another.

The Gym and Shop teachers got made fun of most, probably because they were the coolest faculty members and could take it, and everybody laughed more than the jokes probably deserved. What got the biggest response, though, were the guys from the varsity football team in drag.

After the skits, a few gag awards were given out—to the senior with the lamest absence excuses, to the best talker, the laziest worker, dopey stuff like that—and then Belton came back again. He thanked us all for paying such close attention, for being such a good audience and showing respect to the graduating class of '95. When everybody groaned, he snapped, "Now don't ruin it."

So we shut up.

"Before our show is officially brought to a close and you're all dismissed," he said, "a group of students will lead us in song."

There were more groans that ended abruptly—like four hundred kids were all strangled with piano wire at the same moment—when the Young Patriots, in new bright blue uniforms, marched on stage, then stood in a semicircle behind Will Farmer. One of them had a guitar, which he tuned for half a minute. Then he nodded at Will, and Will leaned toward the microphone. "Please rise," he said, "for our national anthem."

I remembered when it had come on the news, one day two months ago, that the Government had replaced the "Star Spangled Banner" with "God Bless America." Mom was furious, but Dad made a joke. He said it could've been worse. They could've picked a Sousa march. She didn't think that was very funny, though. Me either.

More than half the student body was singing along by the end of the song. I wasn't, but even so, I had goose bumps, I couldn't help it. And my eyes were even a little misty.

After the anthem, Will returned to the microphone.

"I want to thank the senior class for inviting the Patriots to the stage this afternoon," he said, smiling that big smile of his. This was the same Will, I thought, who'd been elected, no sweat, to student government last fall, the same Will who'd been stared at admiringly by girls since the eighth grade, the same Will who'd been my best friend for so long. That great smile. He smiled and asked everybody to give a big hand to the seniors who'd be graduating in just a little over a week. "They deserve it!" he shouted, and led the applause.

He should've stopped there.

But he didn't.

When the clapping died down, he gazed out at us all, only he wasn't friendly-looking anymore, he was somber. "It's been a momentous year for the senior class," he said, "but it's been a momentous year for the rest of us, too—for everybody living in this rich and powerful country of ours. It's been a year of great change"—he paused there for effect, like he'd been taught on the debating team— "and a year of great renewal." His voice boomed and ricocheted off the cinderblock walls, bounced down from the vaulted ceiling.

You could feel electricity wriggle through the gym. Low voltage, but definitely there.

Next to me Mike grew rigid, and I heard him suck in his breath.

"I'm sure," Will continued, "that we've all reflected upon the meaning of these changes, and I know that each and every one of us has felt a deep pride that America has dared to reestablish its cherished traditions of hard work and moral strength, dared to show the entire world that we are ready—and fully able—to lead the way into the future. The American Future!"

There was some mumbling now, some muttering.

"So, before we leave here this afternoon, I think it might be valuable to remind ourselves that in agreement, in unity there is strength. It's been five months since the Great Renewal, five months since the first—and morally corrupt—America was swept away, and I think it would reflect well on this high school if we expressed our patriotism and loyalty by publicly thanking General Sawchuk and the other selfless leaders of this newborn nation of ours—the United Secure States of America!"

Will began to clap directly into the microphone. The Patriots on stage joined him. There was a smattering of applause from the freshmen and sophomores and some halfhearted clapping in back of me.

"Come on!" Will shouted.

And the applause did increase, some, but then suddenly, and I couldn't tell from where came a loud, angry, explosive BOO! That did it. Others joined in, and the booing got louder and angrier and then it was coming from all around the auditorium.

I just sat there, stunned, with mouth shut and hands slack.

And at last all the boos and cheers, catcalling and halfhearted applause diminished and died, and the auditorium was plunged into an awkward, terrible silence. Then somebody sneezed. That broke the tension, and people started laughing. They laughed as though that wet sneeze was just about the funniest thing they'd heard in all their lives.

I watched Will Farmer leave the stage, walking stiffly. Most of the Patriots followed him, but three stayed behind, to glare and to gesture with their middle fingers.

Mike said, "I think the assembly's over."

Chapter 14

Next morning when I came down to breakfast, Dad was sitting at the kitchen table, staring at the steam rising from his mug of coffee. In front of him was the drip pot and a plate of untouched scrambled eggs. I tossed a couple of bran muffins in the toaster, then went back through the house to the front porch for the paper. It was lying on the top step, still in its paper-boy tube. I was bending for it when something caught my eye, and I glanced up.

There were big sparrows on nearly every rooftop. On antennas, chimneys, and gutters. Telephone wires, electric wires, the street lights. Sparrows even in the branches of our chestnut tree.

My throat and mouth went dry, and I tried to swallow but couldn't. I ran back in the house and out to the kitchen, the newspaper crushed in a fist.

Dad said, "Everything's great."

"What?" I sat down heavily in a chair. "What'd you say?"

He chuckled without much humor and pointed at the *Daily Sentinel.* "Everything's great, everything's terrific."

I looked at him like he was nuts or something.

"Forget it," he said. "It's a censorship joke." I'd noticed lately—and especially since Dayton—that he'd been saying that kind of stuff a lot, making wisecracks more and more. He'd noticed a city police car behind us and say, "New Cops following us, Eddie?" Or, like, some letters would be delivered all crumpled up and he'd say, "Is our mail being tampered with? I wish they'd keep the bills." Stuff like that. He only said it to me, though. Never when Mom was around. She wouldn't have appreciated the humor, for sure.

Funny thing was, though, I didn't appreciate it either. For some reason, it bugged me. A lot.

"Mom still asleep?" I asked him now.

"Not asleep," he said. "But still in bed. She doesn't feel like getting up this morning." He looked at me steadily for a couple of seconds, then frowned and glanced away. I went and got my two muffins.

"Dad? Can I ask you something?"

"Sure."

"What's the matter with her, really? I understand how bad all that stuff about her books hurt her, and I'm sympathetic and all, but . . . is she ever going to be the way she used to be? Or never?"

"Eddie." Dad's voice was a sharp, verging on angry.

"Sorry," I said.

He opened his mouth and closed it, then poked a fork at his scrambled eggs. "She . . . I suppose she just doesn't know how to cope with what's happened. She thinks that it's wrong, that all this Moral Renewal stuff is nothing but a fancy excuse for cruelty and repression. She thinks—"

"And what do you think?"

He shrugged. "Well, for starters, I think General Sawchuk ought to find himself a new makeup man. On television he looks like Bela Lugosi."

"That's crap," I said, and Dad looked at me, startled. "That's real crap," I said again, standing up from the table. "You make bad jokes and Mom stays in bed. You're beautiful, the both of you."

Dad was staring at me now with his mouth half open. He wasn't used to me getting angry. But I wasn't, either.

"So what do you think we should do, Eddie? Grab machine guns?"

"I don't know," I said. Then I said, "Maybe," and he grunted, like I was ten years old and was acting stupid or foolish.

"Eddie—"

"Have you been outside today, Dad? Those birds you saw in Dayton, they're here now, they're right outside."

"I saw. But I'm a lousy aim with a slingshot."

"Keep making the jokes, Dad. They're hilarious. You keep making jokes and Mom can stay under the covers, and everything's gonna be just fine. Right?"

I'd gotten so ticked off that I hadn't even noticed that Mom had come into the kitchen. But when I turned to leave, there she was, standing in the doorway with a hurt expression on her face. She didn't say anything, though. Just looked at me, and kept looking at me while I grabbed my school things and left.

Chapter 15

It was early, and if I went straight to school, I'd be there by quarter past eight. That used to be all right, coming in early, but no longer. These days, there were Young Patriots posted at every entrance, and you couldn't hang around outside or even in the halls anymore. You had to go right to your homeroom. The Patriots really thought they were hot stuff and they'd make you show them your student ID, only they called your ID your "identity papers." Let's see your identity papers, they'd say—the creeps! I couldn't believe the Board of Ed had given them charge of the doors like that. Or maybe I could. Maybe now I was starting to believe a lot of things that I just hadn't wanted to believe before.

I walked to Mike's house, hoping to catch him before he left. His grandmother let me in. "Morning, Eddie," she said, then called upstairs, "Speedo, Eddie's here!"

She was a cool lady, Mike's grandmother. Once upon a time, she used to live in New York City, worked in advertising. Doing what I didn't know. She even used to be on the radio. Again, doing what I didn't know. She just slipped those little bits of information about herself into conversations, and I always meant to ask her more about them, but never did. I could be pretty lazy, and it bothered me sometimes.

She and Mike's grandfather had been taking care of Mike and his brother since their parents died.

Sammy was in the kitchen eating breakfast, gobbling cornflakes. He'd surrounded his bowl with half a dozen of his speckled stones. Next to the bowl was a bike decal, which I figured had just dropped out of the cereal box, a premium. "Hey Eddie," he said with his mouth full. I nodded and sat down.

Mike's grandmother opened a can of cat food for her white Siamese.

Two minutes later, Mike came charging in. He snatched up the milk carton and guzzled half the quart, then sleeved away the white mustache. "Ready?" he asked me. Then to Sammy he said, "You coming voodoo boy?"

Sammy scooped up his stones and jammed them in his pocket. The three of us left by the back door.

Now we had to move, or we'd be late, and nobody said anything for a couple of blocks. We dropped Sammy at the John Glenn School and then kept going, really scissoring now. There were birds everywhere I looked, but the weird thing was, I was getting used to them already.

I didn't like that. I didn't want to get used to them.

As we were turning into President Street, Mike suddenly put a hand on my arm to slow me down. Then he said something under his breath.

It didn't register for a second, then it did.

He'd said, "Kantrowitz."

I looked, and it was him—it was Mr. Kantrowitz standing by himself just inside the alley between a dry cleaner's and a Chinese restaurant that had been out of business for about a year. His shoulders were stooped and his hair looked longer, much longer, than before.

When he saw us, he turned and scooted up the alley, glancing over his shoulder again and again, walking quickly but awkwardly, like maybe something was wrong with his leg. Finally, he disappeared.

Mike looked at me.

"It's none of our business," I said.

"Right."

"But let's go."

The alley opened into a concrete courtyard with half a dozen parked cars, but no Kantrowitz. There was a driveway that led out to Monroe Street, so we figured he'd cut straight through and was gone.

But we figured wrong.

As we were turning around to go back down the alley, Mr. Kantrowitz stood up from a crouch behind one of the cars, a green Volvo electric wagon. He scared me, him just popping up like that. And the way that he looked up close kind of scared me, too.

His skin was gray everywhere except where it was bruised, on his cheeks and one temple. His lips were dry and cracked. They looked like Scotch tape that had been picked at. And there was a long, ragged, half-healed cut on his throat.

He stared at us, and we stared back. Then Mike said, "Mr. K, you left us all in the lurch—who won the Spanish-American War?"

I couldn't believe he'd said that, but maybe it was the best thing he could've said, because all of a sudden Mr. Kantrowitz started to laugh. So we did, too. And there we all were, standing in that courtyard laughing about the Spanish-American War. Very strange. And things got stranger.

When Mr. Kantrowitz stopped laughing, his eyes misted. He came slowly around from behind the Volvo, calling Mike Eddie and me Mike. In the past that would've ticked me off, a little, but it didn't now. He told us to listen, and we listened. He said we had to promise never to tell anyone that we'd seen him today, and we promised. "If they knew you spoke to me, they might take you away, like they took me."

"But why'd they do it, Mr. Kantrowitz?" Mike said. "What'd you do?"

"Nothing. It's what I said. I said something to somebody—somebody I shouldn't have trusted." He looked at me. "I made remarks to people I thought I could trust." He laughed bitterly. "You understand?" He glanced down the alley.

"Who?" I said.

He shook his head and wouldn't say. Maybe he didn't know.

"Where have you been?" Mike asked him.

Again, Mr. Kantrowitz shook his head. "It doesn't matter. I'm not there anymore. And after today, I won't be here, either. I'll be gone. But it's all right. I have friends now. It'll be all right. I just wanted . . . I thought I'd like to come back and see the school once before I left." He smiled. "As much as you might think it's crazy, I love that school."

Some shadows moved quickly across the courtyard, making Kantrowitz flinch. We all looked up as several sparrows winged past.

"Mr. Kantrowitz," I said.

"Just be careful. The both of you. All of you. Be careful. This won't last forever. It won't."

"You bet it won't," said a voice in back of me, and I spun around.

It was the Denim Guy.

He was standing with his hands in his pockets, dressed exactly as he'd been that night we saw him at the diner. His gold earring gleamed. He nodded at me, at Mike, then he asked Mr. Kantrowitz, "Ready to go?"

"Quite ready." Then, smiling at Mike and me, Kantrowitz said, "This is . . . this is one of my friends."

The Denim Guy fetched out his pack of cigarettes, stuck one into his mouth, and lit it. From the slack way that he carried himself and smoked, you might've supposed he was just some grown-up gangboy, but his eyes were hard, and smart, very smart, and they never stopped moving, never stopped looking around, looking everywhere. He saw me watching him, and grinned.

Mr. Kantrowitz shook hands with us, then turned and limped off down the driveway, alongside the Denim Guy.

At the end of the drive, he turned and called to Mike, "The United States won the Spanish-American War. The United States of America!"

And then he was gone, and I never saw him again.

Chapter 16

When I got home that afternoon, Dad was in the backyard, relaying one of the railroad ties that he'd put in last summer to make a patio. He was wearing crummy old paint pants and a blue work-shirt with both elbows patched, and he had on a Detroit Tigers baseball cap. He frowned when he saw me, then gave one final shove to the tie and stood up from his crouch. He brushed splinters and dirt off his knees and wiped a sleeve across his sweaty forehead, streaking the grime. We looked at each other for half a minute, then he suddenly turned and walked into the house. So I figured he was still angry at me because of what I'd said at breakfast. Well, tough. There were two sparrows on the roof next door, and if Dad was pissed at me for saying what I felt, then tough.

I went inside and up to my room, put on old

jeans and a Backsliders T-shirt. It was illegal, that T-shirt, but I couldn't have cared less. I took a peek through the window and saw Dad back out in the yard, standing on the patio. Suddenly the muscles bunched across his back and he gave a powerful kick to a railroad tie.

At supper, nobody said anything except pass me this and pass me that. Afterward, Mom disappeared back into her bedroom, Dad went down to the basement, and I sat in the parlor, watching a lousy movie on the VCR. Family life in the U.S.S.A.

Mike called at half-past seven, in high spirits. "How 'bout we take your car tonight?" he said. "My grandfather needs ours."

"Where we going?"

"Surprise."

"What do you mean, surprise?"

"Just what I said, okay? But we're gonna have a good time, guaranteed."

"All right. I'll pick up B.J. first."

"Good. See you in an hour?"

I told him yeah, an hour, then phoned B.J. and told her forty-five minutes. She didn't even bother asking me where we were going.

I wanted to use Dad's Ford, but I didn't want to ask him for it—I was afraid he'd tell me no—so when I was ready to go, I took the Beast.

And as usual, it didn't want to start. I cranked it and cranked it, and finally it turned over, but the engine sounded beat. I hoped Mike's big surprise wasn't a far drive.

I stalled at the light on Adams Street, and stalled

at the light on McKinley, and making the turn from Washington onto Wilson, I stalled again. But that time the Beast wouldn't start. I made a fist and banged the wheel. Called the car a few choice names. Then I climbed out, looked around, slapped my arms against my sides, and started to push.

I was straining and sweating, but the heavy wagon just wasn't rolling very much. Then somebody said, "Hey, let me help," and I looked behind me.

Standing there, dressed in chinos and a T-shirt, was a kid I'd never seen before. About my age, with straw blond hair, freckles, and a small scar on his left cheek, just below his eye. I said thanks as he crouched behind the tailgate and shoved. I was pushing from the driver's door, steering with one hand. Both of us grunting, we managed to get the Beast to the curb.

"Thanks again," I told the kid, and he nodded.

"What's the matter with it?"

I laughed. "The matter is, it conked out."

"Want to look under the hood?"

"Me staring at the engine won't do any good," I said, a little embarrassed. I didn't like people, especially guys, to know I had absolutely no aptitude for automotive mechanics. Sometimes I wondered just what I did have an aptitude for. Sometimes I was afraid I didn't have an aptitude for anything.

"Let me take a look," the kid said.

"Hey, you don't have to."

"It can't hurt."

So I shrugged and reached into the Beast and

popped the hood. He braced it and leaned in and snooped around, ticking his tongue against the roof of his mouth and humming softly.

Half a minute later he grunted, then straightened up and grinned. There was grease across one cheek, and his fingertips were brown. "Try and start it up."

I nodded and slid into the Beast. Cranked it. But the engine only whirred and whirred and wouldn't turn over. The kid said, "Turn it off," and tinkered some more. Then he waved at me to try it again.

And that time it turned over, smoothly.

He stepped away from the hood and folded his arms and smiled at me through the windshield. "Nothing to it."

I left the motor running and got out. "Hey, I really appreciate this."

"Good," he said and laughed. He wiped both hands off on his chinos, then stuck out his right one, to shake. "Roger Stackhouse."

"Eddie Ludlow. Can I give you a lift somewhere?"

"Sure," he said. "Wherever you're going will be just fine."

Huh?

But like I say, I'd never seen him around, so maybe he was new, wanted to make a friend. Which was okay with me. I said I was going to pick up a couple of kids, we were going out. "And you're welcome to come, man."

"Yeah? You sure?"

"Why not? I owe you."

Roger spoke with a twang that wasn't Midwestern, so on the drive to B.J.'s, I asked him where he was from.

"All over. But I was born in Oklahoma, lived there till I was five."

"Yeah, I figured it was someplace like that. So you move around a lot, huh?"

He nodded, then started rambling on about fuel injectors and carburetors, and I listened, not understanding more than one word in five.

When I pulled up in front of B.J.'s house, Roger got out with me.

B.J. answered the door, and I introduced her to Roger, told her about the car trouble. "I was wondering what took you so long," she said. Then to Roger, she added, "That was nice of you."

He made a sweeping bow, like they do in Shakespeare. B.J. laughed, and for just one second I felt a pang of jealousy. I hated it whenever that happened, and it happened a lot.

Then Mr. Pendleton appeared, coming down the hall, pushing his glasses up his nose. "Roger," he called, "good to see you."

Which surprised me a lot.

Roger said, "How are you, Mr. Pendleton?"

"Very well, very well, thanks." But the funny thing was, he didn't look it. In fact, he looked pretty terrible. His face was shiny-pale, and his eyes behind his horn-rims looked bleary, tired. He'd lost a bunch of weight since I'd seen him last. His clothes hung on him like they belonged to somebody else. I wondered if he'd been sick. But B.J. hadn't said anything about that. Come to think of it, though, she hadn't said anything at all about him recently, that I could remember. Mr. Pendleton said, "So, Roger, how's your father?"

"Doing fine."

"You tell him I said hello, would you? Tell him I said hello."

Roger promised he'd do that.

So far, Mr. Pendleton hadn't said hello to me. It was like I wasn't even there.

"You tell your father I was asking for him," Mr. Pendleton said again, like a brown-nose.

If B.J. hadn't finally said, "We have to run, Dad," we might've been standing out there all night listening to Mr. Pendleton tell Roger to tell his father hello. She patted his shoulder and gave him a quick kiss, then winked at me.

Going down the steps I heard Mr. Pendleton shut the front door.

"How do you know my father?" B.J. asked Roger, and he said, "From the Air Force base. I live there."

Chapter 17

"I thought you guys weren't coming," Mike said, pulling open the back door of the Beast. When he spotted Roger, his jaw dropped and his eyebrows jumped. He glanced at me. Mike, Roger; Roger, Mike, I said, and blah-blah-blah. For some reason, Mike wasn't very happy to meet Roger. I hoped he hadn't decided already that Roger was another snob, or something. He was kind of notorious for making snap judgments about people.

"So where are we going?" I asked him. "What's the big surprise?"

He hesitated, then told me, "Take Route 9." In the rearview mirror, his eyes flickered, looked worried. He was sitting hunched forward, directly behind B.J.

"Mike," I said, "where are we going? Really."

There was a long, uncomfortable silence, then

Roger finally said, "Can I make a suggestion, guys? Pull over, Eddie, just for a second."

Something was fishy, for sure. So I did what Roger said, steering to the curb and putting the Beast in neutral. Mike shrugged, and wouldn't look at Roger. "There's a Dark Concert tonight," he finally said, to his knees.

Then his behavior made perfect sense.

He didn't know Roger, none of us did, and that meant we couldn't trust him. And you weren't supposed to tell anybody you couldn't trust about a Dark Concert, ever. Much less take him to one.

B.J. said, "Where's the concert?" but before Mike could answer, Roger said, "I'd rather not know, okay?" He pressed his lips together into an awkward, embarrassed smile. "I think maybe I should get out here. I think maybe that'd be best."

Finally, Mike looked at him. "I hope you understand. I—"

Roger clapped him on the shoulder. "Yeah, sure." He opened his door. "But hey, maybe we can all get together some other time."

"Yeah," I said. "I'd like that. A lot. But hey, I don't want to just let you out here. Can I drop you someplace?"

"I know where I am." He slammed the door, then leaned through my window. "Enjoy the show," he said.

"Big surprise," I said to Mike once we were rolling again.

He took a big breath, exhaled. "Did I know you

were going to show up with some guy we never met?"

"You could've told me what you had in mind. You could've told me."

"Over the telephone? Against the rules."

"All right. So you could've told me this afternoon."

"I didn't know this afternoon. Swear! Richie Vorius came over my house, five o'clock. Look, Eddie, if you don't want to go, we don't have to."

"Who's playing?" B.J. asked.

"Danny Lemon and the Splinters."

"No kidding," I said. Man. A year ago, the Splinters were filling concert halls. Now they were sneaking in and out of dinky little towns like Sandersville. Amazing.

"So, you want to go or not?" Mike asked us, peeved.

"Where?" I asked him.

"Panther Park."

"Let's go," B.J. decided, so I nodded and took Route 9 out of town.

After a while, Mike said, "You know, when you showed up with that guy, I didn't know what to do. I mean, I'm sure he's a cool guy, but, you know."

I said, "Yeah."

"He may be cool and all," Mike continued, "but he's an Air Force brat, right? He lives at the base, right?"

"Just shut up," I said.

Mike flopped back in his seat. "And I thought

you guys were gonna be so happy when I told you about the concert."

We turned off the highway at the billboard for Panther Lake, then rode another couple of miles down a two-lane blacktop. Since we weren't supposed to drive straight to the amusement park, I found a spot a mile away, near the main swimming beach.

There were maybe a dozen other cars in the lot, but we didn't see anybody around. It was dark by then and there wasn't a moon, but we were familiar with the lakeland roads and it took us only twenty minutes to hike to Panther Park.

Ten kids were milling on the gravel outside the gate, which was closed and padlocked and had a sign that said the rides wouldn't open till June twenty-fourth. Nobody was talking. Nobody was smoking. Nobody was drinking. Dark Concerts had very strict rules.

Mike took out three long strips of black construction paper, each of them stamped with a gold clef note.

I took mine, B.J. took hers, then we just waited. Meanwhile, another dozen or so kids straggled up to the gate. There was still no moon, and a breeze was hissing through the treetops. I looked up and spotted some bats. Or at least I thought they were bats.

At last a stocky man dressed in black bib overalls and black high-top sneakers approached the gate from inside the park. He was carrying a long-barreled flashlight, which he trained all around, from face to face. Then he pinned it under his armpit and unlocked the gate.

He didn't speak a word, but collected each ticket and carefully checked it. Then he nodded us the way, and we walked in past the kiddie rides and the game booths and the Haunted Mansion, and finally we saw an open, lighted doorway. The sign on the building's roof said Fun House.

When I was younger, I used to go there every time I came out to the park with my parents. It was huge, like an airplane hangar, with long swooping slides and crooked rooms and trick mirrors and a large, spinning barrel. You could run from one attraction to the next and spend as much time inside as you pleased.

It hadn't changed. Everything was still the same, a little shabbier but still the same, only the barrel wasn't spinning tonight. In an open area in front of the mirrors, though, was a platform stage that I didn't remember. A computerized drum kit, four speakers, three mikes, and a zillion miles of spaghetti wire.

When we came in, there were at least fifty kids standing around or sitting on the floor already, everybody quiet as snow. I saw Mary Doran and her boyfriend, the center on the basketball team, and B.J. waved to the Kelting twins, then as soon as we found a spot we all liked, Richie Vorius appeared, selling concert T-shirts.

"How you guys doing?" he said, then grinned and slowly scoped the Fun House. "Pretty cool place for a concert, huh?" His eyes were pindots, and his fingernails were full of decals: tiny flames and purple skulls, and the old American flag on both thumbs. He nodded and nodded, a kid of few brains. "Pretty cool place." Then he ambled off. Maybe somebody'd signaled to him for a shirt, or maybe he was just wandering, absorbing.

We stood around, sat down, got up and stood around some more, and by the time the doors were finally closed and locked, the place had all filled up. The lights dimmed, and a tall guy with gray hair, pitted skin, and a longhorn mustache climbed to the stage, tested the microphone, and winced at the feedback. "Okay," he said. "Welcome and all that junk. Glad you're here, etcetera." He smiled, showing us bad teeth. Then he shut his mouth and the smile vanished. "Now, listen up. A few precautions, all right? For everybody's protection. We'd love you to clap and cheer and shout your heads off, but you and me know that wouldn't be smart. So no shouting, no cheering, you got it? The band understands, believe me. But if you want to dance, dance. And another thing. The volume ain't gonna be loud as you like it, but under the crappy circumstances, it's the best we can do." He paused, then added, "It's the best we can do this year. But next year—next year, we crank it up. Next year—back in the U.S.A.!"

He jumped down, and two minutes later Danny and the Splinters—wearing skinny bandit masks, just for a laugh—finally appeared and the show started.

My sophomore year, I'd seen the Splinters play Tompkins Arena in Andover and they'd practically blown the roof off. Compared to that performance, this one was silence. Still, it was great to hear some live rock and roll again, and by the third song, almost everybody in the Fun House was dancing, me and B.J. included. Mike just stood on his chair, a big, happy, almost delirious grin on his face.

They played for an hour and ten minutes, no encore, and by the time it was over, everybody was feeling up, feeling sweaty, buzzy, and good. The blood was pumping. And we couldn't help it, when Danny Lemon stabbed his mike back into the stand for the very last time, we had to cheer.

The band split, but the lights stayed down while the doors were opened. We got let out gradually, in small bunches. One bunch would go; then a few minutes later, the next. We left with the fourth bunch and walked, practically on tiptoes, directly to the park gate. There, everybody broke up and drifted off in separate directions.

We cut through the woods, following a curvy dirt path. The moon had risen, but still we could've used a flashlight. Somehow, we missed a turn, and wound up down at Panther Lake beach.

Which, as things turned out, was our bad luck.

Chapter 18

I took my sneakers and socks off, rolled up my jeans, and waded into the water. It was cold and the bottom was mucky with last autumn's leaves. I could hear crickets, and the gnats were out. B.J. swatted a cloud of them away from her face.

Mike had picked up a long, barkless tree branch and was taking swipes with it at the beach grass. "So how was that concert, huh?" Since he'd paid for the tickets, he wanted me to say it was great, so I did, but in kind of a dead voice. I'd fallen into a funk all of a sudden and couldn't figure out how come, exactly.

I came out of the shallows and flopped down in the sand next to the cold remains of a small bonfire—some charred fieldstones, some chunks of wood, and plenty of blackened beer cans bent in half. B.J. came and sat next to me. "What's the matter, Eddie?"

I shrugged, but I wanted to know myself, so I thought about it, and then I had my answer. "Sneaking in to see a concert, sneaking out afterward. You know what I feel? I feel like I'm living somebody else's life, someplace else. This can't be my life."

Mike jabbed the dead branch into the dirt and leaned on it. "My grandmother says that sooner or later, people are going to fight back. She says that's when the trouble's really going to start."

I thought about the demonstration in Dayton, and nodded.

A couple of minutes went by, nobody talking, then Mike crunched down the sand and stood at the water's edge with his hands in his back pockets. "What's that?" he said. "Over there." And pointed.

Across the lake, there were about twenty small and steady red pinpoints, like bright cigarette coals, all of them in pairs. I got up to have a better look. And while we were both standing there, the water lapping around my bare feet and over Mike's running shoes, a bright phosphorescent light suddenly flashed from behind the trees on the opposite shore. It flashed only once. But the red pinpoints stayed lit.

"That's Rhodes's Property," Mike said, and I said yeah, I knew it.

There used to be this guy named Russell Rhodes, a milkman. Lived in a real dump—a spook house—and never spent a dime except to buy land. He'd accumulated almost a hundred acres on that far shore of Panther Lake and surrounded them with rustic fences that said Keep Out. But after he died, there'd never been anybody to chase you, and as kids we'd freely trekked through Rhodes's Property every time we came to the lake.

Mike was saying, "You want to take a hike over there, see what's going on? Maybe Richie Vorius got fireworks."

"It's late."

"Afraid of the Prowler?" Mike joked, and I smiled. Yeah, right, the Prowler. As kids, we'd all been told about the Panther Lake Prowler. He was kind of our local bogeyman. Snatched children, all that stuff. Being told about the Prowler was supposed to keep you from wandering too far away from the swimming beach. "So . . . you wanna go see?"

B.J. had come over. I asked her what she thought, and she said, "Yeah, all right. Why not?"

So we walked all the way down the lakeshore, away from the beach, and then around a cove where the water was topped with gunk and lily pads. Just beyond the cove, we came to the first posted sign. Only it wasn't one of old Russell's, it was a brand-new red-on-white one, on a brand-new chain-link fence. And it said:

STOP
PROPERTY OF U.S.S.A.
ENTRANCE RESTRICTED

In smaller print, it threatened trespassers with a penalty of five years in prison and a fifty-thousand-dollar fine.

We stood there gaping. Finally Mike said, "Since when? Since when is this property of the U.S.S.A.?"

"Got me," I said.

"So what do we do now?"

"What do you mean, what do we do?" B.J. said.

I thought for sure that she meant we ought to turn around and go back. But she climbed the fence, swung a leg over the top, and jumped down on the other side. I stared at her in disbelief, then laughed and scaled the fence next. Mike came last. Grinning at us both, he said, "See what a little rock and roll does to the youth of Secure America?"

Rhodes's Property was still just trees and scrub, trees and scrub. Even Russell's spooky old clapboard house was still standing, every window broken, every shutter dangling. The porch sagged, the paint was blistered, and the front door was missing. We could see straight through the house and out the back.

I didn't know how far we were thinking of going, and I bet neither did Mike or B.J. We walked on through the woods, hunched over a little and moving slowly, carefully, on our toes, like frontier scouts, and it was fun.

Until we saw the second flash of light.

It came from off to our left, from behind a dense stand of oaks on a small hill. It lit the sky and bleached the cloud bottoms. As soon as it flashed, B.J. grabbed my shirt sleeve and wouldn't let go.

I was scared now, but figured if we'd gone this far, we might as well go a little farther. And I tried not to think of that five-years-and-fifty-thousand-dollars stuff.

Sweat begin to trickle down my armpits as we crept up the hill. Near the top, we scrunched down, and kind of duck-walked the rest of the way, then flattened out on our stomachs. I squeezed my eyes shut and opened them, shut them and opened them, trying to give myself better night vision. Then I looked over the top of the hill.

Below, about twenty yards down, all the trees were bulldozed and a freshly made and still unpaved road curved away into a thick evergreen forest. In a bowl-shaped clearing stood two Army convoy trucks and a small tin and cinderblock building. Its windows were dark and part of its roof was missing. Well, not exactly missing—slid back, slid open. Through the opening, I could see a machine of some kind, a smooth, rounded, gleaming thing that reflected the moonlight. On top was a long tube, or barrel, pointing up at a steep angle. I'd never seen anything like it.

Mike took a look, then B.J. did, and when we'd all seen, we just lay on our sides and frowned at one another. Mike started to say something, but I put a finger to my lips. I lifted myself up again, and looked back down, and saw a figure step out of the building, glance once at the Army trucks, then run off into the woods.

That's when I first heard it, a faint clicking

sound, directly in back of us. I twisted around and saw two pairs of those red pinpoints high in some foliage.

And suddenly I knew what they were.

They were eyes.

I scrambled to my feet, dragging B.J. with me downhill, and Mike followed in a crouch.

"Just keep going," I said, "and don't stop."

I wouldn't look up anymore, but I kept hearing that clicking sound. It followed us and got louder. And by then I could hear beating wings.

B.J. half-turned, huffed in surprise, and a sparrow struck her cheek. It soared straight up and looped, looped again, clicking furiously, then returned, its eyes glowing like busy lights. B.J. screamed, and I dove at her, pulling her down just as the bird completed another arc. It flew over us, and a second later I heard a loud snap. Then a whirring sound, then a sparking, finally a sizzle. But no more clicks. When I heard Mike start to laugh, a crazy, scared giggle, I looked around and saw the sparrow lying on a spongy bed of evergreen needles. "The frigger hit a tree—it hit a tree," he said, and I probably would've laughed too—I was feeling insane enough—but before I got the chance, I heard other wings.

Chapter 19

"How long we gonna stay in here?"

I didn't answer Mike. Instead I just crawled across Russell Rhodes's plankboard dining-room floor and raised my head enough to look through a broken windowpane. I could see them all out there in the skeletal branches of a stunted elm, at least ten sparrows, waiting.

There were others in back of the house, on the roof of the ruined chicken coop. We'd checked.

"How long, Eddie?"

"Quit asking me, all right? I don't know." I crept back over to B.J. She was sitting on the floor with her back against the fireplace and her fingers pressed against a cheek. She had a fat welt on her cheek and three bloody scratches on her neck. But what really spooked me, she hadn't said a word in ten minutes, not since we'd run into the house.

I tried to get her to look at me now, but she wouldn't.

"Maybe," said Mike, "Maybe if we just walked away, real slow..."

"Good idea, man. You go first." I reached past B.J. and picked up an iron poker that was lying inside the fireplace. That, plus one gateleg table and a horsehair sofa reupholstered with cobwebs were the only things in the room. I stood up and started across the floor. Mike moved to follow me, but I shook my head no.

I went into the hall, where I could look straight out through the front doorway to the yard. Sooner or later, I was thinking, we had to leave. Because sooner or later, somebody was going to show up. Maybe soldiers, maybe New Cops, but definitely somebody. And probably soon. I slipped across the hall and into what I guess used to be the parlor. Nothing there but some old cartons crammed with mildewed copies of *National Geographic.* I turned around and went out, and as I was edging back down the hall, I heard a sound, a creak, at the top of the stairs. I flattened myself against the wall, and the ancient wallpaper crackled against my back.

When I heard a second creak, directly above my head, I tightened my grip on the poker.

It was definitely, definitely footsteps.

And they were definitely coming downstairs.

Then it was like I was eight or nine years old again, and my throat dried, closed, and every part of me tingled, and I thought, Prowler, it's the Prowler, and he's coming to get me.

I saw a shadow move, and keep moving, and then I saw a man's shape, and when it reached the foot of the stairs, it turned, slowly.

And moonlight through the open doorway silvered the face of the Denim Guy.

Chapter 20

He crouched in front of B.J. then lightly touched her cheek with the back of his hand. She stared at him and didn't blink. He stood up suddenly and pulled off his dungaree jacket and draped it around her shoulders. "You should take her home," he told me, and Mike said, "Yeah, we'd love to."

The Denim Guy smiled.

I started to ask him, "What are you doing here?" but changed my mind and said, "It was you before, wasn't it? That I saw coming out of that building?"

He looked at me and raised his eyebrows. Then he nodded. He walked to the window, bent slightly from the waist, and looked out. "I wonder why they didn't just come in here after you." Then he grunted. "Faulty programming."

I asked him why they hadn't come in after him, but he ignored that. "They're amazing, though, aren't they?" he muttered, almost to himself. "Little spy birds, little bombs. Well, we'll just have to do something about them, won't we?" He turned around and looked at us across the room. "But first we have to figure out where they make them."

"That building over the hill," Mike said. "What was that? Is that where the birds come from?"

The Denim Guy shook his head. "It's what I was hoping. But apparently not. I have no idea what that place is, or what that machine is. But I'm sure we'll all find out eventually, huh?"

We. We'll all find out. We'll just have to do something. We. Was he talking about him and us? Or him and somebody else? I finally came out and asked him, "Who are you?"

"This is going to sound real corny, and I swear it's not my idea. But for the time being I'm supposed to be called Citizen Eighty."

Mike said, "You're right, it's real corny. I like Denim Guy better."

"What?"

"It's what we called you that night at the diner," I explained. "And the day we saw you with Mr. Kantrowitz."

The Denim Guy was nodding, grinning, and I said, "But you still haven't told us who you are."

He reached out and tore at a long cobweb that hung from a ceiling fixture. He shook it off his fingers and watched it drift slowly to the floor. Then: "I'm just some nobody living in the U.S.A. Understand? Some nobody who doesn't live in General Sawchuk's big backyard. And I'm some nobody who's going to keep on living in the U.S.A.

whether the General likes it or not. But right now, I'm somebody who's supposed to find out where the hell those birds are built, so that other somebodies can do something nasty about it."

"Citizens Eighty-one and Eighty-two?" said Mike, and the Denim Guy smiled.

I turned and looked at B.J., watched her eyes narrow, focus, and take sharp aim at the Denim Guy. She was coming around, coming back to earth, and it was talk of the bird factory that did it. I was wondering if she knew that her father was connected to all of this. I'd been wondering about that for a couple of weeks. I'd been too chicken to ask her, though. And still was.

Shc stared at the Denim Guy, then lowered her eyes, lifted a knuckle to her teeth, and bit it. I sat down next to her. "We got to get out of here," I said. "Somebody's gonna show up."

The Denim Guy shook his head. "I doubt it. Not till morning at least. They figure they have the birds, they don't need a lot of sentries."

"You mean there's nobody around? At all? But we saw two trucks. And we saw those flashing lights. Who did that?"

The Denim Guy looked at me, then cocked his head to one side. "Well, there were a few Army guys in the building. You're right. But I wouldn't worry about them anymore. They've been taken care of."

The way that he smiled then gave the creeps, up my spine and down both arms.

I watched him glance through the window one more time, then he strode out into the hall. We heard him climbing upstairs. I asked B.J. how she was, she said okay, all right, speaking around her knuckle. I mentioned stitches, I mentioned hospital, and she said no, no way. I shut up and looked at Mike. He was rubbing a hand slowly across his mouth.

When the Denim Guy returned, he had a duffel bag slung over one shoulder, and he was carrying several small Baggies filled with thick dark fluid. The stuff looked like beef gravy, but I'd seen enough Stu Haring movies to know that it was a gelatin explosive.

Without saying a word, he ripped a small tag off each of the Baggies, then walked around the room, pressing them against the walls. They stuck. "Time to go," he said at last, and before I could ask him how, or what, or anything else, he reached into a pocket and pulled out that small beeper thing he'd taken from one of the New Cops he'd demolished at the Colony Diner.

"Stand out in the hall, all right?"

I watched him thumb a small tablet on the side of the device, saw a blue light wink on, heard a quiet hum. Then he jerked his head at us, and I helped B.J. get up. We went out, and ten seconds later heard a loud rustling sound, wings beating. Through the front doorway we could see all the sparrows leaving the tree.

I looked back into the dining room, and the Denim Guy was leaning against the armchair, and the birds were flying in through the broken windowpanes and bursting out of the fireplace. They settled down, then quit moving entirely.

The Denim Guy used a penknife to slash open the back of the chair, and a disposable lighter to set fire to the stuffing. Then he grabbed up his duffel bag and joined us.

"Just in case any of them took pictures of you," he told us.

"You can control them?" Mike said, amazed.

"Until the New Cops get around to changing the codes," said the Denim Guy, waving the device. "Which they will now."

We followed him out of the house, and when we reached the tree, we stopped to look back at the jumping flames.

We heard the first explosion before we got to the cove. We heard the second and third ones while we were climbing the fence. "Get going now," said the Denim Guy.

I wanted to talk to him more, I wanted to ask him some questions, a lot of questions, but B.J. was already trudging ahead stiffly, walking like a zombie, so I only said, "I think I live in the U.S.A. too."

He frowned. "You think?"

"Yeah," I said. "I think."

"Well, when you're sure, call me."

"How?"

And half a minute later I was running after B.J. and Mike, repeating a telephone number over and over and over in my head, memorizing it.

Chapter 21

We got back around two o'clock, long past curfew. I was praying we wouldn't see a police car. And we didn't.

Mike had been apologizing ever since we'd left Panther Lake, saying it was all his fault that we'd gone to Rhodes's Property. I kept telling him to forget it, but finally I told him, "Shut up." B.J. sat rigidly, a hand on her neck, a fist in a lap.

I dropped Mike, then drove straight over to Truman Street, parked, and shut off the ignition. "I'll walk you in," I told B.J.

"No."

"Yes. I want to make sure you're okay."

"Just go home, Eddie, all right?" She was mumbling, distracted, then suddenly she gave me an angry shove and jumped out. She ran across the lawn, but before she went inside, she whipped off the Denim Guy's jacket and flung it away. I sat in the Beast and ground my teeth. I waited for B.J.'s bedroom light to switch on. I waited five minutes, I waited ten, and it never did.

Finally, I walked over and picked up the jacket and put it on, then I stood below B.J.'s window, tossing up wood chips from the flower bed. I called her name a couple of times. Nothing. So I went into the house. In Sandersville, hardly anybody locked doors.

The hall was pitch black, but I was as familiar there as I was at home, almost, so I didn't bump against anything. Quietly as I could, I climbed the stairs, glided carefully past her parents' bedroom, and then stopped outside B.J.'s.

And heard her crying.

I pressed my forehead against the wall and stood like that for twenty minutes. When the crying stopped at last, I turned around and crept back away.

But I didn't leave. Instead, I walked out to the kitchen, where there was an entrance to the garage. That door was unlocked, too.

Mr. Pendleton's workbench was piled with twenty different cartons and trays, and a pair of enameled containers that resembled extra-large tackle boxes. I switched on an overhead light, then started clawing through everything. There were a few simple tools that I recognized—screwdrivers and soldering irons—and a lot of very tiny electronic doodads that I didn't. I kept telling myself, You're crazy, you're nuts, but I kept rifling stuff anyway. I was picking out something from one of those tackle boxes when the garage door rumbled up.

Mr. Pendleton stood in the driveway blinking at me for several seconds. Then he came charging in, throwing bright glances from side to side. He grabbed the box and slammed the lid down. "Just what the hell are you doing in here?"

I didn't answer him.

He reached across the table and tried to grab me by the denim jacket, but I knocked his hand away. That surprised him: what, Eddie Ludlow?

Wrong: the Denim Guy.

But who was I kidding? My knees felt watery.

"Where's my daughter?"

"Upstairs," I said. "Asleep. Maybe."

"I can't believe you'd just—" He shut up when I stretched out my arm, opened my fist, and showed him the sparrow head that I'd just plucked from his box.

His mouth fell open. "Ludlow, I could get you arrested."

"I'm sure you could. You could also get B.J. killed." I dropped the bird's head on the table. "Your daughter was lucky tonight, Mr. Pendleton. She could've had her head blown off. Thanks to you."

He put a hand to his mouth and his eyes opened wide. Then his hand dropped away, his shoulders sagged, and he stared at me, his lips rubbing against each other.

I walked past him and out through the garage door.

On a rooftop across the street, two lights glowed red on a dish antenna.

Chapter 22

It took me a long time to fall asleep. My temples were throbbing and I kept thinking about the Denim Guy. I'd hung his jacket over the back of my desk chair, and in the dark, all the No!! buttons faintly shimmered.

When I finally dropped off, I dreamed that I was with the Denim Guy, and the two of us were out on Panther Lake in a canoe, an aluminum canoe. It was hot, and we weren't talking as we glided past Rhodes's Property, staying close to shore, skimming lily pads. Then suddenly, from out of the tall trees, which were thick and spread out on top, dozens of sparrows flew up, as though they'd been startled. And all we could hear was clickclickclickclickclickclick . . .

I woke up, and my heart was racing and my

throat was parched, so parched I could scarcely swallow.

It took me several seconds to realize that I was still hearing those clicks.

And that they were in the house. Downstairs.

Clickclickclick . . . clickclickclick.

I threw off the top sheet, listened, still heard them, and my hair bristled. I thought about climbing out the window, shinnying down the rain gutter. I thought about shouting for Dad, calling the Denim Guy's number. I even thought about wriggling under the bed. But what I did, finally, was grab a swimming trophy, hold my breath, and open the door.

Then I leaned over the hall railing. There was a light on down in the kitchen that hadn't been on when I'd come home.

And that's where the sounds were coming from, the kitchen. I skulked down the stairs, like a burglar, and when I reached the bottom, the clicking abruptly stopped. Then started. Then stopped. Then I heard paper crumple, and finally I breathed again.

When I came in the kitchen, Mom was sitting with her back to me at the table, which was cluttered with yellow pads and manila folders, pencils and fiber-tip pens, a cup of coffee, a plate of cherry pits. There was a fresh sheet of paper in her ancient Remington typewriter, and about twenty balled-up false starts in the wastebasket. She was wearing a robe over a nightgown, and she was scratching her head, reading something she'd just written.

Then she realized she wasn't alone, and glanced around. And smiled.

"What are you doing?" I asked her.

"What's it look like? I'm writing."

"A book?"

"Maybe a book, maybe not. So far, it's just writing. But it feels good."

"Yeah?"

She smiled again and said, "It feels very good." Then she said, "Sit down, Eddie. Do you want something to eat? There's coffee."

"No," I told her, "I don't want anything," but I sat. I tipped my chair back and looked at the page number on the paper in the typewriter. Page eleven. "I thought you'd given it up for good."

"Me too. But what you said the other morning—you were right about me. I've just been feeling sorry for myself."

"I never said that."

"You didn't? Funny, that's what I thought I heard you say. And I couldn't stop thinking about it. I have been feeling sorry for myself, I've been feeling sorry for all of us. And, I tell you, Eddie, suddenly the other night, I felt really sick and tired of feeling sorry. I got mad at myself."

We looked at each other for a long time, and I don't know what she was thinking, but I was remembering back to when I was a kid, all the way back to when Mom used to make up stories for me at bedtime. I loved them. They were always about a boy named Eddie, and Eddie got to go to some pretty fantastic places full of wizards, pirates, cowboys, dragons, astronauts, you name it.

Lots of times Eddie wound up a prince by the end of the story. Every time he ended up a hero.

When I was eight or nine, Mom started to write down some of those stories, mostly because Dad kept pestering her to. He said they were good, and so did I. She eventually sold three children's books and had about nine others rejected. But hey, three out of twelve ain't bad! My mother the author. I was so proud. It was great.

Then last March, all three of those books ended up on the New National Culture's X-list, which meant they were yanked out of every library in the country. And you couldn't buy them anymore, either. Her publisher wouldn't even sell her the warehouse copies. Because those had to be pulped.

She'd tried to find out why her books—three harmless little storybooks!—had ended up on that list. She tried for about a month. But nobody would give her an answer, and every day her spirits sank a little more, a bit further. Finally, she quit making phone calls, stopped writing letters, and gave up. Just gave up. Gave it all up.

"What's the new book about?" I asked her now.

"You can read it when I'm done."

"Come on, just give me an idea."

"It's not the most original idea in the world, but..."

"Come on."

"All right," she said. "It's about a boy who finds a door in his attic that was never there before, and he walks through the door into a mysterious country where everybody is unhappy because some bad people have started putting the good people into prison. That's as far as I got. It's a start, though. At least it's a start."

"Yeah," I said, nodding and nodding. "It's a start." Then she went back to work, and I stood up from the table. It was almost four-thirty in the morning by then, and I was so tired I felt dizzy, furry around the edges.

Before I went back upstairs, though, I had to ask her something, just one last thing. "So what's the boy's name?" I said.

And Mom smiled.

Chapter 23

I didn't speak to B.J. again till Monday, at school, where she ate lunch with her girlfriends, not with me, then acted remote and fidgety when I finally got her alone. I asked her what her parents said about the bruise on her face and the cuts on her throat, and she told me nothing. They believed her lie, she said, the one about running through the trees at Lincoln Park and forgetting to duck. "Even your father?" I said. "He believed that, too?"

"Yeah, even him," she said coldly, then made some lame excuse and hurried away. I stood there, baffled, watching her disappear down the corridor. Hadn't Mr. Pendleton said anything to her about catching me in the garage? Hadn't he told her what I'd said? Apparently not. Unless, of course, B.J. was lying to me, too.

It was the end of June, and that was the last full week of school, exam week, and by Tuesday I was too busy to worry much about anything except passing five tests. I saw B.J. every day, and we ate lunch together twice, but she stayed preoccupied, untalkative, worried. I kept telling myself it was just exam pressure. That's all. Exam pressure. I didn't believe it, though.

None of my own exams was too brutal, and English Lit, for a change, was a breeze. Fifty multiple-choice questions and one long essay. On Hamlet, a guy I could sympathize with. He had all kinds of suspicions, all sorts of questions, old Hamlet did, and just wanted to know what was really going on. He bided his time, trying to figure it out. Yeah, but look what happened to him. I figured it was good to be cautious, but if you were too cautious, you could end up stuck full of swords.

So maybe that's why I decided, by the end of the week, to go ahead and call the Denim Guy's telephone number.

A woman answered on the first ring, and said, "What number are you calling, please?" and I told her, "Five-five-five, seven-three . . . eight-zero." The first five digits belonged to my own phone number, and were just fudge; the last two digits meant I wanted to talk to Citizen Eighty. I was just doing what the Denim Guy had told me to do. I was following instructions.

"I'm sorry," said the voice, "could you repeat that number?"

And then I said, "Five-five-five, seven-three-two-seven."

My home number.

"No," said the voice, "you must've misdialed."

Which was what she was supposed to say, according to the Denim Guy.

I hung up then, expecting him to call me.

He didn't.

Saturday evening, though, Roger Stackhouse did. I was surprised to hear from him, but glad, too. He asked me when school was over, and I told him Tuesday. So he said, "You feel like coming out to the base next Friday? Shoot some baskets, play some Ping-Pong, maybe. You play Ping-Pong?"

"A little," I told him. "You know who's good, though? Mike Fromkin."

"So bring him."

I said all right, then I said, "Listen, Roger, about what happened last weekend. I felt bad and all."

"Don't."

"Well, you didn't miss anything"—which had to be the lie of the century.

The following Tuesday morning there was an assembly at eleven-thirty that was over by noon. Short and sweet. And then it was summer.

After I'd cleaned out my locker, I met B.J. and Mike in front of school and we started walking home together. Mike was talking about his job, which he'd be starting on Monday, and I was half-listening and half-watching B.J. Her face was like stone. No expression. I reached down and squeezed her hand. She smiled weakly and squeezed back. Then she let go.

There were a couple of seniors leaning against a Buick Solaris at the corner of President and Fillmore, and as we strolled by, one of them lifted the trunk and gestured to us. I took a peek. The trunk was loaded with albums and laser discs, paperbacks, magazines, video cassettes, rock-group jackets and concert T-shirts, and long strips of fingernail transfers. I shook my head. Mike was too busy talking to even notice.

He wanted us to walk him to his house so we could pick up his car and go riding. "Start the summer right," he said.

That was okay with me. Not with B.J., though. "Maybe next week," she said.

Mike looked at me, then asked her, "You okay?"

"Yeah, I'm fine, just lay off," she snapped, and Mike flinched.

"Hey look, forget it," he said, his feelings hurt.

He was still sulking when we reached his corner. "Well, here's wishing us all a good summer," he said, making it sound like an accusation. We watched him slump away.

"I should've apologized," B.J. mumbled, mostly to herself. The tip of her tongue showed at the corner of her mouth.

"Hey," I said, "he understands."

"Yeah? What's he understand?"

"That you got some things on your mind." I wasn't talking about Mike, really. I was talking about me. And I had the feeling she realized that.

I walked her the rest of the way home, and

knowing what kind of mood she'd been in—what kind of mood she was still in—I didn't really expect her to ask me to hang out. But she did.

Mrs. Pendleton was in the living room, sitting with her feet up on the sofa, when we came in. She was smoking a cigarette and listening to *Fiddler on the Roof.* She loved those old musicals and owned half a zillion Broadway cast albums. Them you could still buy. A cocktail glass and an aerosol can of room deodorizer stood on the lamp table. She nodded to us, then shut her eyes, concentrating on "Matchmaker, Matchmaker." I saw B.J. make a face.

We had root beers in the kitchen, then B.J. kept shaking her empty glass from side to side, making the ice clink. "I wish it was next year," she said all of a sudden.

I looked at her, surprised. "How come?"

"So I could go away."

"You mean away to college?"

"I mean away anywhere. Just away. Far away from home."

She lifted her eyes to mine. "It's really getting awful . . . around here."

"You never said."

She smiled sadly. "No, I never did." She gave a little shrug. "Mom doesn't know what's going on, and doesn't care. She's oblivious, and likes it that way. But Dad . . ."

"What?"

"That stupid job of his. They want him there eighteen hours a day. He's starting to look like an old man. And he's so jumpy, so moody. And now this," she said, nodding toward the backyard.

I got up and looked through the screen door.

Mr. Pendleton, dressed in grungy gardening clothes, was taking listless whacks at the crabgrass with a golf club, a putter.

I turned and frowned at B.J. She moved her shoulders again. "He hasn't gone to work since last Tuesday."

"Why?"

Her eyes began to fill, and she glanced away, wiping them with her forearm. "He went last Monday, but came right home. I don't know what's happening. He keeps telling Mom he doesn't feel like going back. And Mom just acts like nothing's the matter."

My stomach suddenly felt hollow. Then it tightened when Mr. Pendleton trudged wearily up the back steps and into the kitchen. He narrowed his eyes at me and for a second I thought he might throw me out.

But he just said, with an odd, throaty chuckle, "Today I'm playing hooky."

His hands twitched at his sides, and I felt uneasy. B.J. looked frightened. He sat at the table, pushed some hair off his forehead, and began moving his lips, moistening them. I saw him glance at the cuts on B.J.'s neck. They were almost entirely healed, but one looked like it might leave a small scar. He blinked, and moved his eyes to mine. "I just didn't feel like doing the work today. You can understand that, Eddie, can't you?"

I started to nod, but flinched instead when Mr.

Pendleton suddenly chopped at the table, hard, with the side of his hand. "And maybe I won't feel like doing the work tomorrow, either." He winked at me, and my scalp crawled. I didn't know what to say.

When the telephone rang, Mr. Pendleton turned halfway around in his seat and glared at it. It rang and rang.

"That's them calling," he said. "They want me to come in. But—I just don't feel like it. They can live without me at Lab Eleven."

The telephone kept ringing, and I wondered how come B.J.—or Mrs. Pendleton—didn't answer it.

But maybe, I thought, he'd told them not to.

The phone rang so long it started making me nuts. I counted: sixteen, seventeen, eighteen...

It stopped ringing after twenty.

"If you don't feel like doing the work," he said, "you just shouldn't go. Right? Especially if you decide the work isn't worth doing." Then he got up from the table and went back outside.

I stared through the screen after him, and when I looked away, B.J.'s eyes were red and she was sniffling. "He just needs a little time off," she said. "He's been working too hard."

I said, "Yeah, sure, he'll be fine." And I thought, We'll all be fine. But the thing was, I wasn't sure that I believed it.

Chapter 24

I took the long way home, just scuffling along and thinking, squinting up and seeing birds on every wire, looking across the street and seeing a flagpole without a flag, glancing behind me and seeing a dark gray Chrysler Billion turn the corner—seeing a couple of New Cops inside it. I got depressed, so I started to run, which usually helped. Not today, though.

I was still running, breathing like a bellows, when I turned into Roosevelt Street. I cut across my lawn and flopped down on the front porch. Instantly, I was feeling bummed again, so I just let my mind go blank. And that was a big relief.

I guess it stayed blank for quite a while, because I didn't even notice the woman in the gray dress till she was standing right in front of me, smiling.

"You Eddie?" she said.

I looked at her, and she was something. Long brown hair, a narrow, pretty face, and the most amazing eyes. They were palest, palest blue. She looked about twenty-five, and I'd never seen her before in my life.

"Somebody wants to talk to you, Eddie," she said. "I can give you a lift, if you want." She nodded back toward the street, at a blue Toyota with a crumpled-in rear passenger door.

I got slowly to my feet, jumping my eyes from the woman to the car and back again. "Who wants to see me?" I felt a pressure behind my sternum, and my voice sounded a little funny, strangled.

Then she stretched out her right fist and showed me a signet ring on her third finger.

The engraving said: No!!

"How about it, Eddie? Want to talk to him?"

The Toyota had Pennsylvania plates and a crummy muffler and a staticky radio. While we drove down Ridge to North Main, we listened to the two o'clock news—the Official News, the same report that was on every other station across the dial, across the country—and the woman kept making cracks about the newscaster. She said he sounded like a fundamentalist preacher, and it was true, he did. Hey, maybe he was. General Sawchuk saves.

Before last January, it used to bum me out every time I'd listen to the news and it was all bad. But it bummed me out even worse now, now that it was all great, all rosy. Because I didn't believe it.

She pulled to the curb in front of the locksmith's,

then pointed me to the building next door, where the plate window was soaped cloudy and a realtor's for-rent sign was taped to the glass.

We got out and crossed the sidewalk together. She knocked at the door.

The Denim Guy let me in.

I almost didn't recognize him. He'd cut his hair short, and his earring was gone, and he was dressed in a three-piece summer-weight suit. And pinned to the suit's lapel was a 119 button. I started to turn, to run, but he grabbed my elbow, and his grip was like iron.

Chapter 25

"You gotta realize something, Eddie," he was telling me, "and the sooner you do, the better off you're gonna be. And what you gotta realize is this: Everything ain't always what it seems."

He'd closed and locked the door and was standing with his back to it, his arms folded across his chest. I was staring at him. There was absolutely nothing in the store, just carpeting on the floor and some dustballs in the corners. One rack of fluorescent ceiling lights flickered.

The Denim Guy grinned slowly, then he plucked off the 119 pin, dropped it, and stepped on it.

He tipped his head toward the back of the shop, at a curtained doorway. I followed him and the blue-eyed woman into a small white room with three desks. There was a Psyche computer on one, a telephone on another. There was also a trestle table with a coffee machine. Blue Eyes asked me if I wanted a cup. I said no, and she sat down at the telephone.

The Denim Guy sat behind the computer desk and gestured at a chair. "You called the other day. What about?"

Before I could answer, the phone rang, and Blue Eyes said, "What number are you calling, please?" Then she said, "I'm sorry, could you repeat that?" I watched her scribble on a pad of paper.

"Eddie. You called the other day. What about?"

I took a breath and looked at the Denim Guy. Then I said, "I guess I wanted—"

He cut me off. "You guess, you guess. You always guess. Don't you know? You have to start knowing, Eddie." His eyelids narrowed, and his brown eyes gleamed.

"I want to know if you're for real," I told him.

"For real?"

"Because if you are, I want to help. I want to help change things back to what they were before. I want to live in the U.S.A. again."

"Why?"

"Because that's my country. This other . . . thing isn't."

"You sure?"

I squeezed my hands together, I bit my lip, then I raised my eyes and said, "Yeah, I'm sure."

The Denim Guy leaned toward me. "This isn't a movie, Eddie. What's gonna happen is probably gonna happen slow. Freedom takes more than two hours to win."

"Yeah," I said, "I know."

"And we're no big organized movement. So you can get that idea out of your head. We're just starting."

I nodded, and when the Denim Guy didn't say anything else, I told him, "There's something else I wanted to talk to you about."

"I'm listening."

I glanced at Blue Eyes, still talking on the phone. Then I said to the Denim Guy, "I know where the birds are being madc."

He stared at me, surprise becoming a frown, until the corners of his mouth slowly turned up. "Where?"

And I told him: "Harris Air Force Base, Lab Eleven."

He asked me how I knew, and I explained about Mr. Pendleton, and he listened quietly, nodding from time to time, and finally he stood up.

"What do you want me to do now?" I asked him.

"Nothing. But you'll hear from me. Promise."

He walked me back through the store, and we shook hands, and I left. I didn't look back, just walked straight to the corner, then turned down Cleveland Avenue. Parked at the curb, in a no-parking zone, was a Chrysler Billion, and the New Cop behind the wheel watched me steadily as I went past.

Chapter 26

Friday afternoon, I borrowed Dad's Ford and picked Mike up. We drove out Route 9 to Harris AFB, fifteen miles from town.

At the main gate were a pair of sentry booths and a twenty-foot-high fence with razor wire swirled at the top. Half a dozen posted signs said: Stop.

A guard wearing a flapped holster strolled over and peered into the car. He didn't seem much older than me, and he looked almost familiar, like maybe I'd seen him around town. "Hey guys. Come to enlist?"

I laughed and told him we were here to see a friend. As soon as I mentioned Roger's name, he grinned. "The Colonel's kid? Well, if you see the Colonel, you tell him Private Brennan looked alert as he could be." He walked back to one of the sentry booths and hit a switch. The crossarm rose slowly and the gates swung in.

"The Colonel's kid," said Mike.

"So what?" I asked him.

"So nothing. I'm just saying—the Colonel's kid."

When I was younger, my parents used to take me out to Harris for the air shows on Sunday afternoons in the fall, and as we drove through the base now, everything looked just the way I remembered it. The buildings were trim and neat and freshly painted. The grass looked greener than life. The only real difference was the total absence of American flags. Instead, the flagpoles were hung with various Air Force flags and with a number of solid white ones with bright blue 119's on them.

Roger had told me to meet him at the PX, and there he was, standing in the powerful June sunlight. He climbed in the back and said, "Just keep going straight on this road. I'll show you where to park." Then he said to Mike, "I meant to ask you when we met. Are you any relation to Nicky Fromkin?"

Mike said, "Who?"

"The guy who plays drums for the Sunday Orphans."

I glanced at Mike and he had this funny half-puzzled, half-delighted smile on his face. Finally he shook his head and said, "No, no relation."

I laughed, then Roger did, then Mike.

After I parked, we just walked around for a while, Roger showing us runways and satellite dishes, a fitness center, the Officers' Club, blah-blah-blah, then a complex of five residence towers. "That where you live?" Mike asked him.

"No, I live way over on the other side of the base. In a nice house. My father has some perks, you know?" Then he changed the subject quickly, suggesting that we head over to the Recreation Center and get something to drink, play the video games, fool around, have a little fun. We got the message: He didn't want to talk anymore about himself, or his father.

A few minutes later, while we were circling around a huge parade area, I saw the Young Patriots.

There were about twenty of them, dressed in their bright blue uniforms and doing martial drill with rifles hefted on their shoulders. I stopped and stared—goggled, was more like it—and when Mike saw, he grunted in disgust. Roger frowned at both of us. "They're spending the summer out here," he said. "Some sort of training."

Mike screwed up his mouth. "What sort?"

Roger frowned again, then shrugged. "I don't know anything about it. Or them." He turned suddenly and walked on ahead.

As we were coming down the path toward the Recreation Center, I noticed a squat, two-story gray stone building, a ways off to our left. It had barred windows and two guards in front with automatic weapons. I asked Roger what it was.

"Detention facility."

"You mean the stockade?" Mike said.

Roger nodded, and suddenly I was wondering

if anybody inside was looking out at us right now, seeing us pass by, free. I got a shiver.

We went into the Rec Center, got Cokes from a machine, then played some Ping-Pong. Mike was good; he'd always beaten me, sometimes even shut me out. But he was no match for Roger Stackhouse, who held the paddle Chinese-style and played an incredible, lightning-quick offense, firing the ball from side to side, then smashing it right down the stripe. He grinned from ear to ear every time he won a game, and then he reminded me, more than a little, of Will Farmer.

Later on, we shot pool, then ended up in a cavernous game arcade. While I dumped sixteen quarters into electronic pinball machines, Mike and Roger stood around talking about cars and stereo. I was surprised and kind of pleased that they'd hit it off. Maybe Mike figured that if Roger knew who the drummer was for the Sunday Orphans, he had to be okay. Even if his father was a colonel.

Half-past five, we left the Rec Center and started back to my car, Roger taking us by another route so he could show us more of the base. For a guy who'd just moved there, he'd sure familiarized himself with the place fast enough. And he seemed proud of it, too. Air Force brat.

"Where'd you live before you came here?" I asked him as we were crossing the lawn in front of a small aviation museum.

"Washington," he said.

"How long were you there?"

"About a year."

"So you were living there last January."

Roger nodded, then started down a grassy double hill.

"What was it like?"

"What was what like?"

"Oh come on," I said, hearing an edge coming into my voice, and being a little startled by it. "You were in Washington during the coup, what was it like?"

Roger's face darkened. "Coup?" he said. "Is that what it was? Gee, I thought it was the glorious Second American Revolution. I thought it was the start of the great Moral Renewal. Just goes to show you how much I know." He was talking through clenched teeth, and I couldn't tell whether he was being sarcastic or serious, bitter, angry, smug, or what. It was weird.

Finally, he snorted and said, "Actually I wasn't anywhere near Washington last January. I was visiting my mother's folks in Boston. Colonel's orders."

That last remark definitely was sarcastic.

At the bottom of the hill was a compound of three white stucco buildings with dish antennas on the roof and plenty of posted signs on the high, wraparound fence. Authorized Personnel Only.

"Research facilities," Roger explained before we could ask.

Then I said Mike, but he was already looking where I was looking. Already nodding yeah.

"Sure enough," he said, "it is."

So we both started to jog, calling at the same time: "B.J.!"

She was inside the fence, pacing up and down, and our shouting startled her.

"This where your father works?" I asked, and she glanced behind her at one of the white buildings. Then she turned back to me and smiled sadly. "Where he used to work. He just quit." She looked so miserable that I wished like anything there wasn't a locked gate between us. "He's getting some of his things, and I'm—and I'm going to drive him home."

I didn't know what to say. Neither did Mike. Or Roger. It was like we'd just heard that somebody died, almost. Finally, Roger told her, "Well, I'm sure he's found a better job," and I admired him for that. He had smooth, Roger did.

B.J. bit down on her bottom lip, like she was embarrassed, then she turned again and looked back at the lab building. I glanced at Mike, and he gestured with his thumb that we all should beat it, leave her alone. I suppose he was right, it was the right thing to do, so I shrugged and told B.J. I'd call her tonight. The three of us started off again, heading toward the parking lot.

Fifty yards up the pavement, I stopped and looked back. Mr. Pendleton had just come out and was walking over to B.J. His shoulders weren't slumped and he wasn't shuffling. He actually looked like he had some pep. Lugging two cardboard cartons, he strode quickly to the gate and unlocked it. Then he and B.J. stepped through it together.

"Come on," Mike called. "It's almost five-thirty."

I hurried to catch up.

"She's really cute," Roger was saying when I fell into step with them both again.

"Watch it," Mike told him. "She's Eddie's girl."

Roger looked at me. "That so?"

"That's so."

"Then it's so," he said, wistful-like, and nudged me with his elbow.

Two, three seconds later, it happened.

We heard a loud thump, then a gigantic blast. The concussion felt like a defensive end had slammed into me from behind. Penalty! I went sprawling, and tasted dirt. The heat came next, followed by a second explosion. I jumped back to my feet, seeing flames surge and chunks of wood and masonry arc through the air. All around us, things were crashing to the ground, boards on fire, hunks of metal.

One of the buildings in the research compound had blown, and when I realized that, I lost my head and went charging straight back through the oily smoke, shouting and yelling crazily, screaming B.J.'s name.

I couldn't even see the compound now, the smoke was so thick and the sheets of fire so high and wild. A siren went off, and then from every direction, a hundred directions, people came running. I heard another siren blow, then the howl of a fire truck, and I was still running, still calling B.J.'s name. Somebody grabbed me and pinned back my arms, and I was kicking him, and screaming, "Where's B.J.? B.J.!" But the guy wouldn't let go.

Then from out of the sky and falling everywhere, falling all around us on the grass, on the blacktop and the pavement, came the sparrows—plummeting sparrows, sparrows on fire, dozens of them, dropping like stones, sizzling and sputtering and smashing to pieces.

The compound burned and the sirens screamed.

Chapter 27

I was sitting on one of Dad's railroad ties, just staring. It was seven-thirty, a little past. The sun was down and the sky was streaked with pale reds and deep purples. My clothes and hands smelled of smoke.

I heard the screen door open and bang shut, and when I looked around, Dad was standing on the deck. I moved over and he sat down.

"How're you feeling?"

"All right," I said.

He nodded soberly, then we sat there together for a long while, not speaking. You could see the dark moving in, gradually.

"There was nothing about the fire on the news," Dad said finally.

I shrugged.

"That probably means it was pretty bad."

"I already told you that."

"And seeing as how it was pretty bad, they're bound to find somebody to blame, real quick."

I just kept staring at the grass. "You know those birds, the ones you saw in Dayton, the one you see around town?"

He nodded, his eyes tight on my face.

"That's where they made them. That's what blew up today. That's why Mr. Pendleton was quitting his job. He didn't want to make them anymore."

"You seem to know a lot of things, Eddie."

I shrugged.

"And you never told me about any of them. Until now. Afraid I'd make another wisecrack?"

I shrugged again.

"Have you tried calling B.J. again?"

"Only about ten times. Nobody answers. They took her away, Dad. I saw them. The security police took her and Mr. Pendleton."

"At least she wasn't hurt."

"Yeah," I said. "Right."

He stood up. The sky was almost fully dark now, and the moon was a slender crescent. "Let's take a ride. Meet you out front." He went in the house for his car keys.

When he came back out, I was sitting in his Ford, in the driver's seat. He raised his eyebrows. Whenever we went out together he always took the wheel. But he didn't say anything now, just tossed me the keys through the window and climbed in the passenger side. I drove to the corner and turned left on Ridge.

We both knew where I was going.

I drove around Adams to Grant, then swung down into Truman. As we approached B.J.'s house, I saw two cars in her driveway, both Plymouths, and another one, a Chrysler Billion, parked right up on the sidewalk. They all had Government license plates. I got a shaky feeling. "What are you doing?" Dad said when I started to pull over.

"I want to see if they're home yet."

"Keep driving, Eddie."

I looked at him.

"It appears the Air Force already found somebody to blame," he said.

Chapter 28

I was in Mike's bedroom, and for once he didn't have the stereo blasting. He didn't even have it on. He sat on the floor next to his bed, fingers pressed against his temples. "Fine," he was saying, "you want to help B.J.—how?"

I shook my head.

"If this was a movie, Eddie, we'd just go out, find the guy who really blew up that place, and everything would be great. Last time I checked, though, it wasn't a movie."

"I know who blew it up. I think."

Mike looked at me. Then he went over and shut the door. He came back and stood in front of me, scowling. "What?"

I shrugged, then told him about seeing the Denim Guy again, in the storefront on North Main. I told him everything.

"And how the hell did you know Mr. Pendleton made those things at the base?" His eyes were bright with anger.

"I just did."

"B.J. tell you?"

"She didn't know. Maybe still doesn't."

"Then how—"

"Mike, it's not important. What's important is that we get B.J. off that base. Somehow."

"Why didn't you tell me what was going on? I thought we were best friends."

"We are."

"So?"

"So nothing, I just had to figure things, out for myself."

"I could punch your lights."

I looked at him, I looked at the rug. Then I said, "I'm sorry."

He fumed a little while longer then flopped down on the bed. "So the Denim Guy blew up the laboratory and B.J. and her father are taking the blame. I mean, five minutes after he quits, the place explodes. No wonder they think he did it."

"And it's all my fault."

Mike sat up, stared at me, then nodded slowly. "Call the Denim Guy."

"I have. Nobody answers."

"Wonderful."

"We have to get her off that base, Mike."

"Ourselves? Get real. And how do you know she's still there, even?"

"I know it, that's all."

"Okay." Mike sighed. "So what do we do?"

"Go back out there. Now."

"We can't just get in."

"Sure, we can. It's Sunday. Remember when we were kids?"

On the way downstairs, we passed Sammy trudging up. He had a shoebox full of those painted stones and rocks, and he asked us where we were going.

"None of your business," Mike said.

"Can I come?"

"Get lost."

We left, took Mike's car, but didn't drive straight to the base. First we stopped in town center.

We parked a block away from the storefront, then walked back.

Sundays were always quiet in Sandersville, nothing was open, not even the diner, and everybody either stayed home or took a day trip. So it wasn't peculiar that North Main was dead as the cemetery. No, but it was very peculiar to see so many cars parked there, lining the curbs. I counted ten before my gut tightened and I told Mike, "Just keep walking."

When we passed the store, I made sure I didn't even glance at it. We crossed Fillmore, then walked down to the First World War monument and sat on the granite base.

"Bad feeling?" Mike said.

"Too many cars."

"I noticed that. Half of them Plymouths. Air Force."

I nodded.

"What shop was it, anyway?"

"The one with the window soaped up."

He looked at me strangely. Then frowning, he pinched his bottom lip between his thumb and first finger, and tugged. "Eddie . . ."

I watched a sparrow, a real one, settle on the parapet of a brick office building directly across the street. Since Friday, I'd seen very few of the other kind around town.

"Eddie . . . that's the same shop I saw Will Farmer come out of, last month. You remember me telling you he was carrying a couple of boxes?"

"There's more than one empty store in Sandersville, Mike."

"No. It was that one. Right next door to Modern Yarn. It was the same store, Eddie. Believe me."

I shook my head, to clear it. What was it that the Denim Guy had told me, about things not always being what they seemed? Oh, man. I stood up. "Let's go out to Harris, okay?"

So we did, and drove in with a lot of other cars, most of them full of local families. There was a dress parade going on, but we skipped that and wandered over toward the research buildings. But we couldn't even get close. Enlisted men in starched fatigues turned us back. Even so, we got a quick look. The entire compound was nothing but damp rubble, and parked nearby in an asphalt turnaround were several trucks full of debris.

From there, we made our way to the Detention Center. There were two guards posted out front, same as on Friday, and as we ambled past, they looked at us, but without much interest. I wanted to stop and stare at the windows, but didn't. I was sure B.J. was inside. Then I wasn't so sure. But where else could she be?

About forty yards down the walk was a grassy hillside with picnickers. I saw a little kid run over to a trash bin and lob in a soda can.

Mike said, "Well?"

"I'm thinking." And what I was thinking was crazy, totally insane. We couldn't seriously expect to snatch B.J. from an Air Force stockade, but even though it was crazy, I wracked my brains, trying to come up with some kind of plan.

But I'd never been too good at making plans.

Chapter 29

Mom was sitting at the dining room table, writing, when I came in at half-past eight. There were pens scattered around, several legal pads, and a cup of coffee. "You had some phone calls," she told me. "Roger Stackhouse. Do I know him? And Will Farmer, just a little while ago. They both want you to call them back."

Will Farmer?

I phoned Roger and got a woman with a real snooty voice. "Colonel's residence," she said. I asked for Roger, and she told me, "Please wait, I'll see if he's at home."

He picked up, and I said, "You got a maid answering the phone?"

"It's my mother," he said, making me feel like the world's biggest dope. But he was laughing, so

I guessed it was okay, I hadn't offended him or anything.

When he finally quit laughing, all of sudden his voice turned real serious. It reminded me of how Will Farmer's had sounded at the assembly a couple of weeks back.

Funny, that Roger kept reminding me of Will.

"There's something I want to talk to you about," he said.

"Okay."

"Not on the phone. Can I see you tomorrow? Could you come out here? Around eleven? It's important."

The base, again? But I told him all right, yeah, and hung up. Dad had come into the dining room and was sitting at the table across from Mom. They both were looking at me.

"I went to see Mrs. Pendleton before, Eddie," Dad said. "While you were out. She wouldn't answer the door."

I nodded and started to go upstairs.

"Eddie, this'll all work out. It's obvious they had nothing to do with that explosion."

I shrugged, but inside I felt almost sick. Maybe it was anxiety, or maybe it was guilt. I couldn't really tell which.

Chapter 30

Roger lived in a humongous Tudor house that looked like it cost three million bucks. It was in a separate, remote section of the base. Lawn sprinklers were spinning, and security guards were patroling. One of them—a tall, angular guy with small, unfriendly eyes—stopped me before I could turn up Roger's walk. "You lost or something, kid?"

"No," I said, just as Roger appeared, coming around the side of his house.

"It's okay, this is a friend of mine," he told the guard, who nodded, turned immediately around, and strode off.

I looked at Roger, then I looked at the rich house in back of him, the windows golden, catching the late-morning sunshine. "Your father must be some big shot," I said.

"All colonels are," he said, kind of coldly, I thought. "But my father especially, yeah. He's base commander."

I gaped at him. "You never said."

"You never asked."

He led me around to the side of the house, then down into the basement, to a big, square, carpeted room with sofas and lamps galore—the kind you see in ritzy catalogs—a wet bar and a mahogany entertainment center that took up an entire wall. State-of-the-art equipment. I followed him across the carpet into another, smaller room. Framed posters of pro ball players on the wall, a couple of straight-back chairs, a student desk, a stereo, and a small refrigerator. He opened that and brought out two cans of black cherry soda. That's all that was in it. About twenty cans of black cherry. I guessed that was his favorite flavor. Maybe, I thought, I can be a private eye when I get older.

He popped the ring and stared at the foam. Then he said, "B.J. is here on the base, did you know that?"

"I figured."

"What happened Friday wasn't an accident. Somebody put a bomb in one of those buildings. It wasn't an accident."

"So you said."

He frowned. "They think maybe Mr. Pendleton had something to do with it. I shouldn't be telling you this."

"No?"

"Listen, Eddie, I don't know Mr. Pendleton, really, but he doesn't seem the mad-bomber type."

At that I had to smile, which Roger didn't seem to appreciate.

"It looks bad," he continued, after bristling. "I mean, one week he refuses to come to work. Tells his supervisor that his conscience is bothering him. The next week he resigns. And the whole place blows up."

"Can they prove he did it? Or is proof just another thing of the past?"

"The investigation is still going on."

"For how long?"

"I don't know."

"You're the Colonel's kid."

"I was waiting for that."

"Sorry."

"Since she's your girl, I just wanted you to know she's all right."

"How do you know?"

"Come on, Eddie. People don't get tortured in the U.S. . . . S.A."

"I want to get her out of here."

"You can't. So you're just going to have to wait."

"That's all? That's all you wanted to say?"

"What else do you want me to tell you?"

"How about where they keep the key to the Detention Center?" I said, trying to sound half serious, half flip.

"Who says that's where they are?"

"Then where are they?"

"I don't know."

"So how do you know they're okay?"

He filled his cheeks with breath and puffed. "My father told me."

"I have to go."

"Eddie . . ."

"What?"

"I don't like most of what's been going on, either."

"Either?"

He grinned. "You're not so great at keeping your feelings to yourself. You or Mike."

I shrugged.

"I don't think Mr. Pendleton put that bomb there."

I shrugged again and said, "Well, don't look at me."

But he did. In a funny kind of way, he did.

He walked me back outside, and as we were crossing the lawn, a pearl gray limo with two small 119 flags snapping on the hood rolled up the driveway and stopped. The rear door opened, and an Air Force officer climbed quickly out, followed by a heavyset New Cop. They seemed to be arguing, gesturing sharply, and they kept it up as they strode into the house together.

"Your father?"

Roger nodded, then we shook hands, and I told him I'd seem him again real soon.

"It'll be all right, Eddie. When the investigation is over, everything'll be all right."

I gave him a nod, but I was sick and tired of hearing that. All right? Everything was going to be all right? I didn't believe it. Because so far, nothing was.

Chapter 31

On the way back to my car, I stopped at the perimeter of the parade field and stood watching the Young Patriots go through another drill. When it finally ended, they broke rank and ambled slowly, tiredly across the grass and into a long, low cinder-block building.

I shrugged and turned around to go, and there was Will Farmer, grinning at me. He was dressed in a blue sweatshirt with the Young Patriots logo stenciled on it in white, khaki pants, and sun-glasses. The reflector type with bulging lenses, like all the New Cops wore.

I looked at him, then looked away and started to walk, rapidly.

"What's your hurry?" His smile vanished. "What're you doing here?"

"I have a friend out here."

"Eddie, I called you last night. Your mother tell you?"

"What'd you want?"

"I just wanted to talk to you about B.J."

"What about her?"

"Oh, come on, Eddie, give me a break. The less news there is, the more things people know." He pulled off his shades and his eyes blinked in the bright sunlight.

I speeded up, but he just quickened his step.

"This stuff with B.J. and Mr. Pendleton—arresting them," Will said all of a sudden. "It's crazy. I mean, there must've been a hundred people went through that building last Friday. Anybody could've put a bomb there. Even me."

I looked at him, astonished, and he flashed me a small, neutral grin. We'd stopped walking. "You?"

He shrugged. "Sure. I was there for a while. Me and the rest of the Patriots. They gave us a guided tour of the whole base, since we're going to spend the summer out here."

"Then why aren't you in the Detention Center?"

"Why would they suspect me, or any of the other Patriots? We're above suspicion. When you're above suspicion," he said, "you almost have it made."

I looked at him, then wagged my head from side to side. "I don't know you anymore, Will."

"Sure you do. I'm still the same guy who used to be your best friend. Who couldn't wait to grow up and be a Great American. You're just not seeing me." He winked before putting his shades back on. Then he turned abruptly and strode off, across the parade ground.

Chapter 32

The next day was the not-so-glorious Fourth of July. No municipal parade or picnic, no red, white, and blue bunting, no flags, and everybody with a job went to work, including Mike.

Mom left the house around eleven and came back at noon with hot dogs and hamburgers, fresh corn, and a bag of charcoal. Then she called Dad, who was making prints in the darkroom, and he came right upstairs and started a barbecue fire. I was kind of proud of them both for thumbing their noses, a little, at General Sawchuk, but I was too bummed out to take any real pleasure in what they were doing.

Bummed, and angry, and I was angriest at the Denim Guy. Where was he? He'd promised to get back in touch with me. He'd made a promise, then broke it.

Well, screw him, I thought. I can deal with things myself.

Maybe.

Roger Stackhouse telephoned at twelve-thirty. "I'm in Sandersville," he said. "At a Mobil station on South Main. Can you give me directions to your house? I have to talk to you again."

"What's the matter?"

"Just give me directions, all right?"

I was waiting out front when he arrived not five minutes later in a dark blue '95 Pontiac. "You want to have something to eat?" I asked him, but he shook his head, so I climbed in the passenger door. The upholstery smelled showroom-new, and there was less than five hundred miles on the odometer. A mini-TV was mounted under the dash. Nice car. But who cared? Roger looked pale.

"Things are happening at the base, Eddie. I don't know everything, but it doesn't look good for B.J. The New Cops have taken charge of the investigation."

Maybe I'd gotten used to big bad surprises, maybe I'd reached the point where I was expecting them. Because as Roger talked, and talked excitedly, I sat there cool as butter, just listening. To his telling me that he'd overheard—yeah, all right, eavesdropped on—his father talking about the lab bombing with that New Cop we'd both seen, and that the New Cop had ordered Colonel Stackhouse to release the "two new prisoners" into his custody. The Colonel didn't want to, Roger said, but the New Cop insisted.

"Can he do that?" I asked Roger. "I mean, your father's in charge of the base."

"First there's General Sawchuk, Eddie. Then the rest of the Joint Chiefs. Then come the New Cops. Everybody else comes after."

"Okay. All right. So what happened, finally?"

"My father told him he could have the prisoners."

"And the New Cop took them? B.J.'s gone already?"

"No. Tonight. The New Cop's returning tonight."

"Where are they going?"

Roger looked at me, bleakly. "Nowhere."

"Nowhere? You mean, they're staying at Harris? Well, at least—"

He cut me short. "You don't know what I'm talking about, do you? Nowhere is a place, Eddie. It's where the New Cops interrogate special enemies. It's where a lot of politicians and federal judges ended up, and military personnel who wouldn't serve Secure America. Nowhere is a place, Eddie. A bad place."

"In Washington?"

Roger shrugged.

I pushed a hand through my hair and slumped down in the seat. I could see a haze of cooksmoke drifting out from my backyard. "Special enemies? B.J. is a special enemy? Did the cop say anything about her?"

"No. He never even mentioned her by name. Or Mr. Pendleton, either. But it's them he wants.

He kept talking about the two suspects in the Lab Eleven bombing."

"They're leaving tonight? By plane?"

"Car."

I looked at him, and immediately he said, "Eddie, don't even think about it, don't even think of rescuing her. There's nothing we can do."

I smiled at him, for saying we, at least.

Then I started wracking my brains. For a rescue plan.

Chapter 33

That night, before I drove over to Mike's, I tried the Denim Guy's number one last time.

And somebody answered.

But when the somebody—a man, not Blue Eyes—asked for my name, I cracked down the receiver, then stood beside the phone, feeling dizzy.

"Eddie—you okay?" Dad used the remote to freeze the TV picture, then he and Mom stared across the room at me. "What's going on?"

"Nothing. Really."

He looked so grim, so concerned and serious that I almost wished he'd make some wise remark. Almost wished. I scooped up the car keys from the hall table, then threw them a wave, and ran out. When I was getting in the Ford, I glanced back. Mom and Dad were watching me through the window.

I didn't know when I'd see them again.

Or if.

But I didn't want to think about that.

Mike was in his backyard, watching Sammy throw stones from a supermarket carton at a bunch of soup and tuna fish cans that he'd set up on the brick barbecue. It was almost dark, and whenever he whipped a stone, it looked really neat—a bright blur of fluorescent color whizzing through space. He was a lousy shot, though, and the stones kept missing their targets and plopping in the grass. But he didn't have any problem finding them again. Because they glowed.

"Ready?" I asked Mike.

"No," he said. "But let's go."

"You can change your mind." I'd picked Mike up at work earlier and told him about Roger's news. And about my plan. "Really, Mike. You don't have to come."

He shook his head. "I'm coming. I'm crazy, but I'm coming."

Finally—whack!—Sammy hit a can. He whooped, then shouted, "Hey guys, I just destroyed the Golden Gate Bridge."

"Destroy yourself," Mike said instinctively, then he frowned and said, "Hey kid, loan me and Eddie a couple of those stones, would you? We could maybe use a little magic."

Sammy looked surprised, then cocked his head, waiting for another insult.

When it didn't come, he said, "Sure, Mike, sure—what colors you like best?"

Chapter 34

We were sitting in the Ford on the plaza of a service station at the crossroads of Route 9 and the base road. The station was closed, which was good, since we'd been there for over half an hour already, parked alongside a lighted telephone booth. When I'd come out this afternoon to get the phone number for Roger, I'd gotten a fill-up, since I had no idea how far we'd be driving tonight.

We were listening to the Sunday Orphans tape, but I'd told Mike to play it low. I wanted to hear the phone when it rang.

He was beating his index fingers on the dash, and I was cleaning my fingernails, again, with the pin on the back of a No!! button.

"Eddie?"

I restuck the button.

"Eddie, you're not suddenly going to change the plan, right? We're just going to follow them, right? Not do anything else?"

I nodded.

"I'll go anywhere—I'll even go Nowhere—with you, you know that. But promise me we're only going to follow them."

"I promise."

And even though I was wearing the Denim Guy's jacket, I meant to keep my promise.

Roger called the phone booth at nine twenty-three. Exactly.

"They're leaving," he said.

"You saw them?"

"Right this second I'm standing in the rec hall and watching them pull away from the Detention Center. They should pass you in a couple of minutes. A black Billion, Pennsylvania license plates. Two cops in front, B.J. and her father in back."

"You saw her?"

"A girl and a guy, in handcuffs, yeah. And two cops."

"Thanks, Roger."

"I don't know what you think you're gonna accomplish."

"I'll know where she is."

"Yeah, I guess. Call me when you can, okay?"

I promised, and hung up.

Chapter 35

"What if Nowhere is, like, in Colorado? We gonna drive to Colorado?"

"They're traveling east, Mike."

"Okay, New Jersey. Are we going all the way to New Jersey?"

"I told you, man, you didn't have to come."

"I'm just asking."

"Let's just concentrate on keeping them in sight, okay?"

There was a Mitsubishi moon van between us and the Billion, which we'd been following now for something like forty-five minutes. Sandersville was back there, way back there.

"Eddie, I've been thinking. What if the Denim Guy is dead? That's not possible? You had that bad feeling about the shop, like it was being watched. Then nobody answers at the number he gave you. Then somebody does, but wants to know your name. What do you think?"

"I think we're turning."

Without signaling, the Billion cut into the exit lane for Galina and Morgantown. I followed, and then we were on the Stallion Pike, a fancy name for a two-lane country blacktop that dipped between corn and tomato fields. The roadsides were staked with reflectors every hundred yards.

Traffic was light. To say the least. Now and then, a pair of highbeams would sweep around a curve then cut to low, and a slat-sided truck would pass us, heading south, out to 9. The Billion had accelerated, but I kept us at fifty. Bugs kept getting smashed against the windshield.

I was trying to figure out why they'd come this godforsaken way, if maybe there was a connection in Galina for the Ohio Turnpike. But I was pretty sure there wasn't. And then I was wondering if here, if someplace out here, was Nowhere.

That didn't seem very likely—I'd been picturing a huge complex with high prison walls and machine-gun turrets—but then, nothing that had happened lately seemed very likely. A year ago tonight—this time exactly, last Fourth of July—I was goggling at fireworks, going ooh and ahh. And look at me now.

"Eddie, check out the rearview mirror."

I glanced there, but didn't see anything, just empty darkness. But Mike was turned around in his seat, kneeling up and facing back, so I looked again, and now I saw it.

There was a car behind us, maybe a hundred

yards back, and it was coming up fast without any lights.

"You think maybe Roger missed that one?" Mike yanked the tape out of the cassette player and threw it under his seat, like it was dope. "Maybe it's another bunch of New Cops, Eddie . . . maybe we should turn off someplace? Eddie?"

The dark car pulled suddenly out into the oncoming lane, and when it passed us, I cringed, expecting—I don't know what I expected. To be forced over, maybe. Run off the road. But no, the car just kept going, then veered back into the right lane, ahead of us, and sped on.

Pennsylvania tags.

Mike laughed, embarrassed. "Sorry," he said. "I thought for a second it was—"

In the tunnel of our headlights, we watched a figure pop its head and torso through a hatch in the roof of the dark car. The figure swayed, struggled to hold steady, then lifted a rifle. We heard two pops, one right after the other. Brakes squealed, and the Chrysler Billion, with a rear tire blown out, skewed off the road, bumped across the gravelly shoulder, and plunged sideways into a cornfield.

The dark car screeched and shimmied.

By the time I could tromp on my own brakes, the dark car had stopped, three or four people had leaped out, and the shooting had started.

Chapter 36

Mike and I were about twenty yards down the road shoulder, crouched behind my Dad's Ford. There hadn't been an exchange of rifle fire in ten, fifteen seconds, but there was a powerful, choking odor of gasoline mixed with something else—maybe gunsmoke, I didn't know—drifting over us. We could hear crickets, and somebody groaning. There was a scurry of movement alongside the dark car. I saw a flash of light, and windshield glass shattered in the Chrysler.

I felt like I was going to be sick. B.J. was in that cop car, in the crossfire.

"Eddie, let's get out of here," Mike said desperately. Then he said, "Eddie, where you going? Eddie! You promised!"

I scuttled into a ditch that ran along the shoulder, then pushed into the cornstalks, which came up to my shoulder. I dropped to my knees, flopping forward, and snake-walked, slithering on my belly. I couldn't see a thing. The shooting was hot again, and I crawled steadily through the field, toward the Chrysler.

Don't think, I kept telling myself. Don't. Just move. But slow, careful.

I couldn't believe this, any of it. I couldn't believe I was here, doing this. (Doing what? And what the hell was happening, anyway?) But I was here, and all that couldn't-believe-it stuff was just more thinking, and I quit it, finally. I had trouble breathing, though, and what breaths I took were so full of gnats I wanted to gag.

Once more, the shooting stopped, abruptly. I heard a heavy thunk, a car door maybe. Then a single pistol shot. Then it was quiet again. Except for crickets. Heat bugs.

I got to my knees, then crouched, then rose slowly, and through a weird grid of stalks, leaves, and husks I saw the Chrysler.

Both passenger-side doors were open, their black enamel streaked with moonlight. And there was a shape, a bulk, a silhouette—a New Cop, armed with a rifle—squatted on the ground between the doors.

A rabbit bolted through the stalks, startling me. I flinched, lost my balance for half a second, and staggered, instinctively flinging up an arm.

Two seconds later, there was a shot that cut corn tassels and peppered my face with them. I dove, then scuttled as fast as I could. Dove again. But scrambled right up, running madly, in a crouch.

The continuous gunfire in back of me sounded like a full-scale war now, and I didn't know if everybody was shooting at me, or if nobody was, or what.

I just kept running, then suddenly I wasn't in the cornfield anymore, I was out in the open, and I froze stupidly, like a buck deer on the highway. The rear deck of the Chrysler was, like, two feet away. I'm dead. The thought was clear, precise, a dull, tired murmur in the back of my skull. I'm dead. I heard a crack, then a loud buzz, and a blurred figure suddenly moved behind the car door.

I'm dead.

But then there was another crack, another shot, and the figure arched, spun around, and keeled over backward. I hit the ground hard and came up in a crouch, pushing off with my toes and diving again, just to keep moving. I felt a bright, digging pain in my leg. I kicked. Heard a cop grunt. He was under the car. I kicked a second time, tried to squirm, roll free, but couldn't.

Then he was on top of me, pinning me, pressing a thumb into the hollow of my throat, and I saw a spurt of light. Then I couldn't see anything. Couldn't breathe. My hands were flopping, beating the ground. Fingers spread, fingers clenched.

He was going to strangle me, and I was going to die.

He kept pressing, pressing, using all of his weight, and I don't know how it got there, man, I don't know how it got from my jeans into my fist—by magic, right?—but somehow I was holding that stone of Sammy's, a blue and orange and green thing the size of an egg, and with all the strength I had left I smashed it against the Cop's nose.

And broke it.

He screamed in pain, his nostrils spurting blood, and he keeled back, off me, and then I was gasping, a hundred small bursts of flak swirling in front of my face. I struggled to my knees, lifting my eyes, and was looking straight into the backseat of the Chrysler.

B.J. wasn't there. And neither was her father.

But the Denim Guy was. The Denim Guy and the girl with the pale blue eyes.

Then I felt the warm muzzle of a gun touch the side of my head.

Chapter 37

What happened next, happened quick.

The gunners from the dark car—three out of four; one had been grazed in the arm—pushed the Chrysler Billion deep into the cornfield, then doused the upholstery with gasoline and set it on fire. They dragged a cop—the one they'd wounded when he tried to shoot me—over to their car and dumped him on the backseat. The other cop—Bloody Nose—they stuffed in the trunk and slammed down the hood. The Denim Guy, freed of his handcuffs, barked out orders.

I ran back up the road to the Ford, and when Mike saw it was me, he stood up from a crouch behind the rear bumper. "Eddie . . ."

"I'm okay."

"B.J.?"

I shook my head, and his jaw dropped. Then

he took a swing at me, but I sidestepped it, grabbing his forearm. "Everything's all right," I said. "Just—"

Car tires squealed, and we both spun around, and the dark car was moving like a bullet down the Stallion Pike. The cornfield was burning, the smoke roiling up, blocking out the moon. Two figures were jogging down the road shoulder, coming at us.

The Denim Guy shouted, "Let's go!"

And the four of us piled into the Ford, the Denim Guy up front with me, Blue Eyes in back with Mike.

It was twenty minutes later, at seventy miles an hour, before anybody spoke.

The Denim Guy looked at me (in the dashlights I could see that one side of his face was puffy and bruised, that his lips were swollen), and he said, "You're nuts, kid. But you're all right. Welcome back to the U.S. of A."

Chapter 38

He'd been looking for something, a landmark, and when he spotted it finally, a bowling alley—Master Lanes—in a town called Foster, he told me to pull in. About ten other cars were parked around back. "Now," said the Denim Guy. "Do you mind telling me what you were doing following us?"

"I didn't know you were the prisoners. I thought—"

"That we were the girl and her father?" He moved his head up and now, catching on. "Friends of yours?"

"You met her," I said.

He looked at me, frowning. Then he nodded his head again.

"But how'd you know the New Cops were taking anybody off the base tonight?"

"How did your friends from Pennsylvania know?"

He smiled. "Okay. Maybe we should both keep a few secrets. For now."

"You could've been killed in all that gunfire."

"Better that than ending up Nowhere," said Blue Eyes.

I looked at Mike in the mirror. He was sitting with his lips pressed tightly together, staring straight ahead.

I turned back to the Denim Guy. "When were you arrested?"

"Sunday morning. They found that little doohinky I took from the cop at the diner, they found some explosives." He gave me a little grin. "It was lucky that Air Force security got us first. If it'd been the New Cops, we would've been Nowhere by Sunday afternoon."

"It was you, then," I said. "That blew up the lab."

He narrowed his eyes. "Not me personally."

"Who?"

"Someday maybe he'll tell you himself."

"Who?" I said again. "Who will?"

But the Denim Guy only shook his head. "In time," he told me. "In time." He cranked down his window and leaned out. A man was approaching. My gut tightened, but then I recognized him as somebody from the dark car, the one who'd put the gun to my head.

"Ready?" he asked the Denim Guy.

"In a second." The man nodded and walked away, disappearing, around the side of the bowling alley. I could hear jukebox music, and a sudden clatter of pins.

"We have to go, Eddie. And I don't think we'll be back."

"But I want to help."

"You have. And will again. There's plenty to be done."

"But what? How? I just can't, I mean—by myself, I can't."

And Mike said, "You're not by yourself, man."

"He's right," said the Denim Guy. "You're not. There're others in Sandersville. You'll find them. Or they'll find you. Sooner or later."

He opened the passenger door and got out, then stood in the parking lot waiting for Blue Eyes. I remembered that I was still wearing his jacket, and started to shrug it off. But he saw me, and shook his head. "It looks good on you, Eddie. Keep it." Then he put his head back through the window. "Be careful, promise?"

Then, just before he went away, I asked him, "Do you know a guy named Will Farmer?"

One side of his mouth turned up, then immediately turned down. He waved and said, "Just be careful."

He and Blue Eyes drifted off together. We watched them go, and a few moments later, heard a car start.

I looked at Mike. "I'm sorry," I said.

"What for?"

"Come on, you're pissed at me. For trying to play hero."

He shrugged. "Forget it."

"Really?"

"Really." Then he laughed and said, "You do nice work, Eddie. For an amateur commando."

We sat there, quiet, a few more minutes, then went into the bowling alley. It was going on two in the morning. Mike got us sodas from a vending machine, while I used the telephone.

Dad answered on the second ring.

"Where are you?"

"I'll tell you when I get home. But I—"

"Eddie, we've been waiting for you all night."

"I'm sorry."

"No, no—we just wanted to tell you the good news. They released B.J. and Mr. Pendleton. With an apology, if you can believe that. They admit they made a mistake. And Mr. Pendleton can even have his job back. Assuming he wants it. They got the people who did the bombing."

My whole body sagged in relief. Mike saw my face and asked, "What, what?"

"I'll be home in about an hour and a half," I said. Then I asked Dad, "How'd you find out? About B.J., I mean. Did she call?"

"No, but we've spoken to her. Your mom called the Pendletons after we got the news from Will."

"From Will?"

"Will Farmer. He called to tell us at nine-thirty."

I said, "But how—" then didn't finish. There'd be time later for questions and answers. Time later to find out who was on our side, really, and who wasn't. Time to find out more about the Denim Guy, about the New Cops, about Nowhere. About

Will Farmer. But right now, it was just time to feel good, and hopeful. A little hopeful.

I hung up, and Mike and I walked back to the car to look at a road map. Because we weren't about to drive home the same way we'd come.

I was feeling a little buzzy by that time, so Mike took the wheel, and as we were driving through a little town, some little Ohio town whose name I didn't know and never found out—as we were passing through there at two-thirty in the morning, I looked out my window and saw a crowd of people standing in an open field. Suddenly there was a burst of colored light, then another, another, and another. Blue and red and white lights tinted the clouds and made streamers.

It was already the fifth of July, but who cared? The fireworks looked beautiful.